HORSE IN THE HOUSE

My father stopped in the doorway and gave us a funny look. 'Did you hear that?'

'Hear what?' I said, trying to keep the horror from my face.

'I didn't hear anything,' said Eliza.

'Hmm,' my dad said. 'I could've sworn I heard—'

There was another whinny from the larder, but this time I was ready. I instantly started coughing.

Eliza started coughing, too.

'Are you girls OK?' my father asked.

'Fine,' I hacked. 'Just a tickle in my throat.' We both kept coughing until we couldn't cough anymore.

'Whew,' I said. 'Must have been something in the air.' Hiding a horse in the house was going to be a lot harder than I thought!

The Animal Rescue Squad series

The Animal Rescue Squad

Horse in the House

by Ellen Weiss
and Mel Friedman

RED FOX

The authors would like to thank:
Scott and Elaine Taylor, Encore Farms,
Cross River, New York.
Dyrdra Martin, a Level Eight gymnast.
The American Miniature Horse Association.

A Red Fox Book

Published by Random House Children's Books
20 Vauxhall Bridge Road, London SW1V 2SA

A division of Random House UK Ltd
London Melbourne Sydney Auckland
Johannesburg and agencies throughout the world

1 3 5 7 9 10 8 6 4 2

First published in the United States by Random House
Inc., New York, and simultaneously in Canada by
Random House of Canada Limited, Toronto 1995

THE ANIMAL RESCUE SQUAD is a trademark of
Random House, Inc.

Red Fox edition 1998

Typeset in Bembo by
Palimpsest Book Production Limited,
Polmont, Stirlingshire

Printed and bound in Great Britain by
Cox & Wyman Ltd, Reading, Berkshire

Papers used by Random House UK Ltd are natural,
recyclable products made from wood grown in sustainable
forests. The manufacturing processes conform to the
environmental regulations of the country of origin.

RANDOM HOUSE UK Limited Reg. No. 954009

ISBN 0 09 971871 5

Contents

Trouble at Havencrest Stables

Picture this:

I'm on the balance beam, doing a front walk-over, and it's going well. Every move is perfect, I'm strong and confident, the crowd is roaring – when I look down and find I'm wearing a tutu! A bright pink tutu! Suddenly the entire audience is laughing. I try to cover myself up with my hands, and then I start to lose my balance. I'm going to fall . . . I can't concentrate because somebody in the crowd is calling my name, softly and then louder –

'Abby! Abby Goodman! Time to wake up!'

I awakened in a cold sweat. It was that dream again, the one I'd been having for months. I hugged myself in my pyjamas, trying to get all the way back to the real world.

My father opened my door a crack. 'Abby? Honey? Are you up? It's 5:45 already. You're going to be late for practice if you don't get a move on.'

Well, there was no arguing with that. I sat on the

1

edge of the bed, blinking. 'OK, Dad,' I said. 'I'm up. I'm up.'

'Breakfast in ten minutes,' he said.

This was one of the mornings, one of the many mornings, when I seriously questioned the whole idea of doing gymnastics. If I was just a normal kid with a normal life, I'd be snoring away right now. Maybe I'd get up at about ten and watch some daytime TV, or go and see a friend. After all, it was summertime. The pressure was off, right? Wrong. For me, summer just meant I had a lot more time to work on my gymnastics.

In the moments when someone was putting a medal around my neck or handing me a trophy, and the crowd was yelling and whistling, it felt as if gymnastics was the best thing in my life, worth every minute. But those moments were few. In between them, there was hard work, pain, frustration, and lots of waking up in the dark.

Don't get me wrong. I'm not just a gymnastics robot or something. I have a lot of other stuff in my life, too: school, horse riding, a little modelling, and, most important, my friends in the Animal Rescue Squad. I don't think I could get through life without Eliza, Lisa, and Molly.

But as far as my father is concerned, nothing in my life is as important as gymnastics. 'It's what makes you special,' he's always saying to me. 'It's a talent that God gave to you, and you are *obligated* not to squander it.'

And as my coach, Rudi, always says in his cute

Russian accent: 'Childhood? Who needs a child-hood? I didn't have one, and I didn't miss it.'

I brushed my teeth and ran down the stairs, fully awake now. My father was pouring the juice.

'What time will you be home today?' he asked me. He's a computer consultant, and he tries to arrange his schedule so he can be home when I get there.

'Probably about four,' I said, chewing my toast. 'Don't forget, I'm going riding after gymnastics.'

My father frowned. 'I wish you'd just concentrate on gymnastics, Abby.'

'We've been through this over and over,' I said, sighing. 'As long as I do my five hours of practice a day, I can do other stuff. Horse riding is *fun*, Daddy. It helps me to just forget about everything. And you promised I could keep doing it.'

'I know, I know. It's just that with this Animal Rescue Squad business now, I'm afraid you're getting too scattered, forgetting about what's really important.'

'Don't worry. You'll never let me forget.' That was about as close as I'd ever got to talking back to him. I got up and took my plate over to the dishwasher, wishing, as I so often did, that my mother was there to cool things off between us.

We cleaned up silently after breakfast, and then it was time for me to leave. He handed me a five-dollar bill for lunch. 'Do you want me to drive you over to the gym?' he asked, not looking at me.

'No, it's OK, I'll walk,' I said.

3

He put his arms around me. 'I'm sorry if it seems like I push you too hard sometimes,' he said. 'It's just that I want so much for you.'

'I know, Daddy. I know.' I kissed him on the cheek and turned to go.

'Fish Surprise for dinner,' he said, and we both laughed. Fish Surprise was frequently on the menu. He was such a terrible cook that what came out of the pot was always a surprise.

Practice went well that day. I spent most of the time working on my beam dismount, and I made a lot of progress. Rudi even gave me one of his rare compliments: 'You could only do it a *little* better.'

I felt good by the time I was doing my end–of–day stretches. I couldn't wait to get on Petunia, my favourite horse at Havencrest Stables, and ride, ride, ride.

Before I started the mile walk to the stable, I stopped off at the small grocery shop near the gym to buy myself a late lunch and a bag of carrots for the horses. I always tried to bring them some apples or carrots, because it was fun to feed them and also because they all seemed to be a little skinny to me. I loved the horses at Havencrest, but I wasn't so crazy about the owners, Sam and Janet Avery. They both were kind of mean and crabby. And I didn't really like the way they took care of the horses.

When I got to Havencrest, I didn't see the Averys around, so I went into the stable. The horses began nickering softly when they saw me; they knew I'd have a treat for them. I went down the line of stalls, feeding each horse out of my hand. But I saved the nicest carrot for my special buddy, Pegasus.

Pegasus was a miniature horse, and he was the cutest little guy you could ever hope to see in your life. He'd just been born in April, so he was only about four months old.

When I got to Pegasus's stall, he made this funny face at me that he always made, pulling his upper lip back and showing me his teeth. I made a face back at him and offered him his carrot. 'Hey, you little funny-face,' I crooned as the colt scoffed down his carrot and then nuzzled my hand. 'I missed you. Did you miss me?' He was so tiny he only came up to my waist. He was no bigger than a large dog.

Pegasus stamped his dainty little hooves and swished his tail. He was a palomino, a beautiful butterscotch colour except for his cream-coloured mane and tail. When he was full-grown, he wouldn't even be three feet tall at the shoulders. He'd never be big enough to ride, except maybe by a small toddler. His only value, really, was his adorableness.

Brett the handyman came in behind me, making me jump. He was always so quiet.

Did you ever have a crush on somebody who was so much older than you it was totally ridiculous? Well, that's the way I felt about Brett. I knew it was stupid, and I could never admit it to anyone. But he was *so* cute. He had this soft brown hair that went into this little dip in front and sideburns – nothing big and icky, but just right. He had the bluest eyes

I've ever seen, a crooked little smile, and muscles in his tanned arms. But he was in college, so I'm sure he thought I was only a little twerp.

'Hi, Brett,' I said. 'Where are Sam and Janet?'

'They're in the office,' he said. 'There's some kind of trouble today. Bad stuff.' I knew he didn't like them any more than I did, but he would never say it. Another thing about Brett that I liked was that he was a very quiet person, very private. He just did his job and didn't talk much. He did whatever needed doing around the stables, from grooming to feeding to painting fences.

'Maybe I should take Petunia out and not bother them. I'll stop by before I leave.'

'Sure,' he said, adding his quick little smile.

He went out to finish cleaning the water troughs, and I started saddling up Petunia.

The office was on the other side of the wall, and normally voices didn't carry through. But today they did, because the voices were being raised. It wasn't that I was *trying* to listen, I just couldn't help it.

'I'm telling you, Sam,' said a man whose voice I didn't recognize, 'you owe me for six weeks' worth of feed, and I'm getting tired of waiting. When are you going to pay me?'

'I'll pay you as soon as I can pay you!' shouted Sam. 'What do you want me to do, *make* the money?'

'I know you owe Frank Herbert a couple of months' rent on the stables, too. I don't know what you're doing with your money, but you sure aren't paying your debts.'

'What I do with my money is my business!' yelled Sam. 'I'll pay you!'

'If you don't, I'm going to have to come back with the sheriff and take some of your horses as payment. I'm warning you,' the man shouted back.

'Don't you threaten me!' said Sam. 'Now get out! I'll have your money tomorrow!'

'You'd better,' said the man. 'I can't keep supporting you forever.' A moment later I heard a car door slam and a car screech out of the yard.

Then I heard Janet's voice. 'If you didn't keep losing all our money on horse races, we'd be able to pay our bills!' she scolded her husband.

'Don't you start with me, too!' Sam retorted.

I'd heard enough. I felt as if I was eavesdropping, even though I wasn't really. Trying not to feel guilty about what I'd heard, I quickly tightened the girth on Petunia's saddle, led her out of the barn, and rode away.

An hour later, when I was finished, I put Petunia back in her stall and walked around to the office door, even though I didn't want to see the Averys.

I stuck my head in hesitantly. Janet was in there alone, working on the ledger at the desk.

'Um – Janet?' I said. 'I've finished riding. You can charge an hour to my account.' I paid for my riding time out of my own money, which I made modelling, because it cost my father a fortune for my gymnastics lessons. That was the deal I'd made with him. I had to pay the Averys at the beginning of each month for the time I was going to use that month. I still had about five hours to use up in August.

'Fine,' she said, not looking up.

'Well, bye,' I said.

She didn't reply.

I backed away, and then hurried out of Havencrest Stables as fast as I could. *Yuck*, I thought to myself. *That was creepy*.

Meeting Night

That night, I wasn't thinking about Havencrest Stables. Something special was going to be happening after dinner, something I was really looking forward to. For the first time, it was my turn to have the Animal Rescue Squad meeting at my house.

After I'd helped my dad clean up the dishes (the surprise was that dinner was actually edible), I asked if I could be excused. Then I ran upstairs to my room and dug around in the bottom drawer of my chest of drawers, until I saw the flash of red I was looking for.

There it was: the Sacred Red Sock. This was a large and fuzzy sock that had become the property of the Animal Rescue Squad during our first mission, when we saved Miss Hanson's kitten Sebastian from an awful death by drowning. The sock had sentimental meaning, and Miss Hanson had given it to us as a token of her gratitude. We'd decided that the sock would become our special, secret thing and that we'd take turns being the Keeper of the Sock. The idea was that whoever had the sock that month would have the meeting at her house. And if there was an emergency, like an animal in need of rescuing, you could hang the sock out of your window to alert everyone that they had to come round straight away.

This meeting wasn't in any way an emergency, but I wasn't going to miss my first chance to hang the Sacred Red Sock out of my window. I opened my window a few inches, pushed the sock most of the way out, and closed the window firmly on the toe. There. That sock wasn't going anywhere.

Then I sat down on my bed to wait. I knew it was only 6:40, and the meeting wasn't supposed to start until 7:00, so everyone could finish dinner. But I was just too excited to do anything but sit there and watch the clock.

The Animal Rescue Squad meant a lot to me – a *real* lot. When, a year ago, my dad and I had moved to Dormouth, a city on the coast of Massachusetts, I hadn't known a soul there. My dad had explained that it was a good idea to move because there was a really great gymnastics coach here – Rudi. There was another reason, too: nobody here knew about my mum, so we wouldn't have to put up with any questions or people's funny looks. Everything my dad said made sense.

But it was agony moving: leaving my friends,

my school, my big bedroom, the riding stable I knew so well. And when I got to Dormouth, despite my father's promises that I'd make friends in an instant, I didn't make any friends at all. I think people thought I was stuck-up because of my gymnastics and my modelling. And so, for the first time in my life, I became really shy. I couldn't just walk up to people and say, 'Want to be my friend?' So I pretended that I was so very absorbed in all my things that I didn't need any friends. They didn't need me, I didn't need them. I probably looked totally stuck-up. But inside, I was hurting. I was hurting badly.

Then one day I bumped into Eliza Spain in the waiting room of her mother's veterinary office. We'd started talking, and Eliza had invited me to hang out with her and Molly and Lisa (they weren't called the Animal Rescue Squad yet). Eliza is about the nicest person you could ever meet in your whole life. She worries all the time – about hurting people's feelings, or doing the wrong thing, or just anything at all she can think of to worry about. But she's the kind of person who should worry *least* about hurting people's feelings, because she never does. Eliza is tall and skinny, and she has very, very frizzy brown hair that she tries to wrestle into a pony tail. She has thick glasses that she can hardly see without.

At two minutes to seven, Eliza rang the bell. She's always on time, because being late is one of the things she worries about.

I ran downstairs to get the door, but my father had got to it first. 'Hi,' she was saying to him. 'I'm Eliza.'

Dad didn't say 'Hi' back. He just pointed the way up the stairs.

'C'mon up to my room,' I said. 'We'll have our meeting up there.'

As we climbed the stairs, my dad called up behind us: 'You're not going to let this go on too long, are you? You have to be up very early in the morning, Abby.'

I sighed. 'No, Dad, we won't.'

Five minutes later the bell rang again. It was Molly and Lisa. They live near each other, so they had come together.

Molly Penrose and Lisa Ho are about as opposite as two human beings can be. But somehow their friendship works OK.

Lisa is like a human tornado – always in motion. Sometimes her mouth is a little ahead of her brain, and she says things that she might not say if she thought about it for a minute. Sometimes her temper gets her into hot water. But she's totally honest. She's not scared of anything, and she has a big heart. She wears the coolest clothes: black or orange leggings, long colourful shirts, big sweatshirts, sparkly trainers, second-hand stuff. Her long black hair reaches all the way down to her behind.

Molly, on the other hand, isn't at all interested in being the centre of attention. She's interested in

12

the Truth. She's very serious. Sometimes she can drive you nuts, because she doesn't mind spending twenty minutes getting something explained to her until she really understands it. But once it's in her mind, she never forgets anything. She even remembers things from when she was two.

Molly is a great person to have in the Animal Rescue Squad. She loves to do research and she's really organized, unlike the rest of us. She looks kind of like the way she is – no nonsense. She has straight brown hair, wire-rimmed glasses, and sort of nice but normal clothes.

Once we were all in my room, we got as comfortable as we could. Lisa and I sprawled out on my bed, Molly sat at the desk (of course), and Eliza lay flat on the floor because she had strained her back helping her mother pick up a Saint Bernard. Eliza helps her mother a lot around the office, and sometimes we go along, too. Even cleaning out the cages is fun when you don't have to do it all the time.

'I wish I could draw horses as well as you,' said Lisa, looking at the pictures I had hanging on my walls.

'They're all I can draw,' I said. 'You're a good artist all around. But I just draw horses because I love them so much.'

'I like that one of the horse rearing up,' said Eliza from the floor.

'That's Petunia – my favourite,' I said. 'She's the one I ride. I sketched her last month.'

'I think we should call the meeting to order,' said Molly, looking at her watch.

'OK,' I said. 'I'm the one with the sock, so I guess I'm supposed to do this, right?'

'Right,' said Molly.

'This meeting of the Animal Rescue Squad is officially called to order,' I said.

Molly mumbled out loud while she wrote the minutes in her small, neat book: 'Meeting called to order, August 14, 7:14 PM.'

'Gosh, Molly, I think it might be 7:15,' Lisa teased. Everybody always teases Molly about being accurate all the time.

'Nope,' said Molly, unruffled. 'My watch says 7:14, and my watch is right. I always check it by the radio in the morning.' Molly has no sense of humour. But we love her anyway.

'Anybody have anything new to report?' I asked.

'That stray cat my mother picked up is about to have kittens,' said Eliza. 'We'll have to help find homes for them in a couple of months.'

'I'll design some nice flyers,' Lisa volunteered.

'And we can all spread the word,' added Eliza.

'Anything else?' I asked.

'We need the treasurer's report,' said Molly.

'Oh, right,' I said.

I scrabbled around in my desk drawer for the battered notebook that Lisa and I passed back and forth as co-treasurers. Neither one of us was very good at keeping records. It was a wonder we kept them at all. I know Molly disapproved.

14

'Let's see,' I said, trying to read my awful handwriting. 'It looks like we have . . . $35.84.'

'We're rich!' said Lisa.

'Yeah, it's because we had that cake sale last month to help out that lady who was taking care of the sick heron over in Westminster. But then it flew away.'

'Oh yeah, I remember,' said Molly.

'Now,' said Eliza, 'I have a possible problem to report.'

We were all ears.

'It's sort of an animal problem,' she said. 'But it's mostly a mean–little–boy problem.'

Everybody groaned. 'The worst,' said Lisa. 'Which mean little boy is it?'

'It's *two* of them,' explained Eliza. 'And they're living right in my house.'

'Eeek!' we shrieked.

She told us that her parents had been thinking for a while about having somebody move into the basement flat of their gigantic old house. Eliza's mother's veterinary surgery is in one wing of the house, and the flat is below that. Eliza had taken me in there once to look around. It seemed as if somebody with imagination might be able to make it into a sort of nice place, but it was awfully dark.

Eliza's parents had finally found somebody to move into the flat. It was a woman named Mrs Pletzer and her twin eight-year-old sons, Stinky and Mike. 'She actually *introduced* him as Stinky!'

15

Eliza marvelled. 'His real name is Antoine. Can you believe that?'

'*Is* he stinky?' Lisa asked her.

'Very,' said Eliza with a shudder. 'The mother seems kind of tired out. They're both covered with dirt, and they have no manners. They're mean little monsters. They like to torture insects when they think nobody is looking.'

'Eeew,' I said. 'And they're right in your house.'

'I'm going to try to ignore them,' said Eliza.

'If you need help,' said Lisa, 'you can call up the Eliza Rescue Squad. We'll deal with them.' We all nodded in agreement.

After that, the meeting pretty much wasn't a meeting anymore. We just flopped around my room, talking about whether Lisa should have her ears pierced, and who we wanted to get for teachers next year, and who the stupidest boy in the sixth grade was. We were just getting to the stage where we were laughing over nothing until our stomachs hurt when my father came up the stairs.

'Time to break it up, girls,' he said. 'Abby has to get up early to practise in the morning.'

Eliza, Lisa, and Molly jumped up. 'Oh, sorry, Mr Goodman,' Eliza said. 'We didn't know it was getting late.'

As they rushed to gather up their things, Molly opened her notebook to write one last thing in the minutes: 'Meeting adjourned, 9:11.'

And then they all went down the stairs and were gone.

Fifteen minutes later, I was ready to go to sleep. I pulled the red sock in from the window and climbed into bed.

Abandoned

The next day was Saturday, the last day of the week at the gym. Sunday we got to rest. Of course, Rudi made up for it by working us extra hard on Saturdays: hours of running, sit-ups, press-ups and kicks. I thought it would never end. And then there was the work on my routines, and he didn't let me get away with one tiny mistake. By the time I was finished for the day, I was achy and tired.

I thought about going home, but I had started the day determined to go riding in the afternoon. I knew I'd feel good once I got on Petunia. I pointed my feet towards the stable.

On the way, I stopped at the shop to buy the usual bag of carrots for the horses. As I passed the counter where they had the coffee-maker, I noticed a bowl full of sugar lumps for people to put in their coffee. I stuck two of them into my shirt pocket. Pegasus deserved a snack.

As I got close to the stable, I noticed that something seemed a little different, a little off. I couldn't figure out what it was. I kept walking.

There wasn't any movement. That was it. There was no hustle and bustle of people moving around the stableyard, or in and out of the office. Just dead stillness.

And then I heard it. It was a high-pitched horse sound, a sound that was almost like screaming. I could just barely hear it, but it froze my blood. I broke into a run.

There was nobody at Havencrest Stables. The cars and trucks were nowhere to be seen. They were gone, all gone. No people in the office, no people anywhere. I ran into the stable and past empty stall after empty stall, following the sound. I knew it was Pegasus.

He was in his stall, the last one, all by himself. When he saw me, he stopped screaming and just stood there, shaking all over. I ran to his side.

'Pegasus! You poor little baby! Did they leave you here all alone?'

I could hardly believe what I'd found. The Averys had packed up and left. Everything was gone! Why? Then it hit me. They'd probably sneaked off in the middle of the night so they wouldn't have to pay their bills.

Those dirty, rotten – I couldn't even think of a word bad enough. How could they do this? They'd taken away my beloved Petunia. And they were going to leave Pegasus here to starve all alone! I had heard stories of people doing that, but I could never really believe it was true. Pegasus wasn't any use to them. He was only a pet. They couldn't make any money from people riding him, and they didn't want to feed him. So they just threw him away like rubbish.

I knelt beside him, stroking his nose, hugging him, trying to calm him – and myself – down. I reached into my pocket and took out the sugar lumps, and he snuffled them hungrily out of my hand. He was shaking a bit less now.

My head was in a whirl. What would happen to him? Who would take care of him now that he was abandoned? Where would he go? It would be dark in just a few hours. I had to figure this out.

Maybe the animal shelter could take him in.

No, it was only open till noon on Saturdays. Besides, even if he could go there, he'd probably be in some little cage next to a bunch of barking dogs. He'd be scared to death.

I kept stroking him. It was hot. The only sound was the buzz of the insects in the fields around the stable. Or maybe it was the buzz in my head, I couldn't be sure.

I noticed that his water bowl was almost empty, so I stood up. 'You have no water left,' I said to him. 'We have to get you some.'

When I started to leave the stall with the bowl, he stuck right to my heels. 'You don't want me out of your sight, do you?' I said to him. 'Well, I can't blame you.' I let him clop along as I crossed the barn to the water tap.

I had just put the bowl on the ground below the

tap when I heard a footstep behind me. I gasped and jumped about a mile.

'Sorry, Abby.' It was Brett, the handyman.

I tried to catch my breath as my heart banged in my chest. 'It's OK. You just scared me.'

He looked around, squinting. 'They're gone. I had a bad feeling that something like this was going to happen.' He looked down at Pegasus sadly. 'They told me to take the day off. In the whole time I've worked here, they've never let me do that. I was kind of spooked, so I came over. They left this little one, huh?'

'It looks that way. He had no food and almost no water.'

Brett just shook his head in disgust.

'What are we going to do with him, Brett?' I asked him.

'I don't know,' he said. 'I live in a little bedsit in town. I don't think I can have a horse in two rooms.'

'I guess not.'

'Why don't you take him home? You can take care of him just fine.'

'My father would never let me have him,' I said.

'Your father doesn't know what a great little horse he is. I bet when he sees Pegasus, he'll change his mind.'

I sighed.

Pegasus nuzzled at me. 'Oh, I forgot your water,' I said. I turned on the tap and he drank thirstily as the bowl was still filling.

I was thinking about what Brett had said. Maybe my father *would* change his mind. A miniature horse wouldn't be living in the house, wouldn't need to be walked like a dog, didn't really need much care at all except feeding and watering.

Thank goodness I know something about horses, I thought to myself. My mother was a rider, and she had started taking me out with her before I could even remember, when I was about three. She showed me how to take care of horses as part of our riding times together. *If she were home now*, I thought –

But what was the use? She wasn't home now.

I went back to trying to figure out what to do about Pegasus. I could pay for his feed out of my modelling money. I had a couple of hundred dollars saved up already. All he needed was about a cup of grain twice a day – that wouldn't cost too much. I'd gladly pay for Pegasus's upkeep instead of paying for riding. Besides, I couldn't ride Petunia anymore now that the Averys had gone.

Could I really keep him? In my mind, I went over all the problems I could think of.

What if I had to go away? If I had to go to a gymnastics competition for a couple of days, I knew my friends would help take care of him. Or I could board him at Eliza's mother's, or find someone else who had horses.

Did we have enough room for him? I thought we did: we had a very big back garden, with plenty of room for him to play in. He could

22

eat his fill of grass in the summertime. We even had a tool shed that he could go into when winter came. I'd heard of people keeping miniature horses in back gardens. Maybe, if I thought of solutions for every possible problem, I could talk my father into it.

Right now, though, I had to make a decision. It seemed to me that there was only one decision I could make. Brett couldn't take Pegasus home, and Pegasus couldn't go to the animal shelter. I *had* to take him home.

I remembered that there was a pay phone against the wall near the office, so I dug some money out of my pocket. I knew I wasn't going to be able to do this alone. I needed the Animal Rescue Squad to help me.

I left Pegasus still drinking beside Brett and went to call Eliza. I knew she'd probably be home. I remembered that Lisa and Molly had talked about going out bike riding together today. But Eliza tried to practise her tuba every afternoon, even in the summer.

Eliza's big brother Pete answered the phone, and I could hear the tuba honking in the background. 'Just a minute, I'll get her,' he said.

The tuba playing stopped, and Eliza came to the phone.

'Eliza,' I said, 'I need your help. There's a horse in a crisis.'

'What? What's happened? What's wrong?' she said, panic-stricken.

'Oh, sorry, don't worry. It's a crisis, but it's not a *crisis*. The horse isn't hurt or anything.'

'Whew. Don't scare me like that.'

I apologized again, and then told her where I was and explained to her about Pegasus. 'I can't leave him here,' I said. 'He's just a baby. He was only weaned from his mother last month.'

'I bet he's cute,' Eliza said.

'He's *so* cute,' I told her. 'Wait till you see him.'

'Well, I guess you can't leave him there all by himself. But what's your father going to say? He doesn't want you to have any pets, right?'

'I'm hoping that if I can just bring him home, when my father sees him, he'll change his mind.'

'What if he doesn't change his mind?'

I hadn't thought that far ahead.

'Maybe my mother would let me take him,' Eliza mused. 'I don't know how the dogs would get on with him, though.' Eliza had three dogs, named Big, Little, and Archie. 'And also, I don't know anything about horses.'

'I'm just going to hope my father says yes,' I said. 'I really want to keep him.'

'O-K,' said Eliza, in that doubtful Eliza-like tone of voice she has. 'So, what do you want me to do?'

'Could you meet me here?'

'How soon?'

'Like now?'

She sighed. 'I guess I can finish my practising later.'

24

'Thanks!' I said. 'You won't regret this.' I gave her directions to the stable, and she said she'd come over on her bike.

After I'd hung up, I went back to Pegasus and Brett. Pegasus had perked up. Now he was frisking around the yard, looking for fun. As I watched him, I remembered that Janet had told me about how Pegasus was the name of a winged horse in a Greek myth.

Brett had to leave. 'I have to go and buy a newspaper,' he explained. 'Gotta start looking for another job.' I said goodbye to him and shook his hand.

'I'll keep in touch,' he said as he walked out of the yard. I hated to see him go.

A New Home for Pegasus

While I waited for Eliza, I took Pegasus out into the field so he could munch on some grass. He was really starting to act like his old self now. He would run towards me, then veer off at the last minute. He made that funny face I loved so much as he skidded past me.

As I stood and watched him, it really hit me. He was mine. I had to take care of him. I was in charge of him. Most kids my age had maybe a gerbil or some small animal to take care of. But a horse? I knew my father wasn't going to help out with Pegasus's care – if he let me keep him at all. Watching him now, I felt scared. Was I up to doing this?

Finally, Eliza pulled up on her bike. 'Sorry it took so long,' she called to me. 'I got lost. I think I took a wrong turn by the petrol station and—' She stopped short as she saw Pegasus, and squealed with delight.

'Oh my God, he's so *cute!*' she said. 'Why didn't you tell me how *adorable* he was?'

'I did,' I said. 'You can't believe it till you see him, that's all.'

'You *have* to take him home.'

She stood her bike against a post and ran into the field. When he saw her coming, Pegasus ran over to meet her. She bent down and stroked him on his flank, and he rubbed his head against her leg.

'I'm in love,' she said.

He wheeled around and trotted across the field.

'I don't know how your father can say no to this,' she said.

'He can say no.'

'But when he sees how much you want Pegasus—'

'When he sees how much I want Pegasus, he'll remind me about how much I'm *supposed* to want to be a great gymnast.'

We sat down in the damp grass and watched Pegasus trot around the field.

'*Do* you want to be a famous gymnast?' she asked me.

'I don't know. I want to make my father happy. And I love to do gymnastics. But I need to have a life. I want to have some fun. I can't just practise all the time. If that means I'm not going to be a great gymnast, it's OK with me. But I *want* Pegasus.'

'Well, then, go for it!'

We watched him for a few minutes longer, and then we got up and brushed our behinds off.

'How are we going to get him back to your house?' Eliza asked.

'Maybe you can walk your bike, and I'll lead Pegasus.'

'OK.'

I went into the barn and looked around to see if the Averys had left anything I'd need for Pegasus. They had pretty much cleaned out anything that was worth much, but I found an old grooming brush on a shelf in the corner. On the floor there was a halter that looked as if it would fit Pegasus. I'd need to buy a hoof pick to clean out his hooves. He could eat the grass in my garden until it snowed, but I'd need to get him some feed pretty soon as a backup. For now, at least, I could lead him home with the halter.

I went back outside and found Pegasus nuzzling Eliza. 'He's a little like my dogs,' she said. 'He's so sweet. I didn't know horses could be so sweet.'

'Miniature horses are really friendly,' I told her.

We set out for home, Eliza walking her bike and Pegasus clip-clopping along beside me. After a while, I turned and looked back at the deserted Havencrest Stables and sighed.

'Is your dad home now?' Eliza asked me as we walked past the park.

I had to stop and think.

'I'm not sure,' I said. 'I think he had to do some errands. I don't know if he'll be back yet or not.'

'Maybe we should think about the best way of presenting Pegasus to him.'

'Well, Pegasus shouldn't just be there when he walks in,' I said. 'Maybe I ought to get him used to the idea slowly.'

'How about if we sort of sneak out the back and put him in the shed for now. Then, after we talk to your dad, we could show him Pegasus.'

'Good idea.'

It was a long walk home. I was really feeling achy after my long day, but Pegasus was having a fine old time. He pranced along the street, his head held high, his nostrils flaring.

Every now and then we'd meet somebody who was outside working on their lawn or about to go out. People kept saying the same things:

'Oh, he's so *cute!*'

'What is it? Is it a real horse?'

'Is he going to grow to normal size?'

'What does he eat?'

Everybody wanted to stroke him, and that was just fine with Pegasus. But it took us over an hour to get home.

At last we were there. Eliza hung back with him while I went to check things out.

'The coast is clear,' I called to her. 'My father's not home yet. We can go around the back to the shed.' I was relieved that we wouldn't have to worry about my dad looking out of the window and seeing us.

The shed was an old, small wooden building. We didn't use it for much except some tools of my dad's. It had a door with a broken lock and two windows, which would be good for making sure Pegasus got enough air. Even in the wintertime, the windows would need to be left open. With a lot of difficulty, I opened them as wide as they would go.

There was a tiny room inside the shed, and it looked just perfect for Pegasus. If he stayed in there, he wouldn't get into any trouble with the tools.

I found a large plastic bowl that would be perfect for water. Eliza ran and filled it up using the hose behind the house. 'There you go, little guy,' she said, putting it down in front of him. 'Drink up.'

The room didn't have a door, so I looked around the shed to see what I could use. Leaning up against one wall was an old door that looked as if it had been inside the house at one time. I put Pegasus into his little stall, and then dragged the door across the entrance. It was really heavy, so I knew that if I could lean it up against the doorway, Pegasus would never be able to knock it over. The height was perfect. He could see very nicely over the top, but he wouldn't be able to jump over. It would do fine until I could rig up something better.

'Well, Pegasus, there you are,' I said with satisfaction. 'Your new home.'

He whinnied at me from inside.

I stroked his neck. 'Eliza and I have to go back in the house now. This is where you're going to hang out. OK?'

I hated to leave him, but I knew he'd be all right.

We went into the house to wait for my father.

Ten minutes later, we were sitting on the dining-room floor playing Sorry when I heard the front door open.

I could tell by the way he slammed the door that my father wasn't in the greatest mood.

'Abby!' he yelled before he'd even crossed the living room. 'Your stuff is all over the place! How many times do I have to ask you to put your shoes and socks away?'

It was worse than I thought. He appeared in the dining-room doorway and took in the scene. He did not look thrilled.

'Hi, Mr Goodman,' said Eliza.

'Hi,' said my father.

On a sudden impulse, I jumped to my feet. 'Dad,' I said, 'could Eliza stay for dinner?' I didn't want to be alone when I broke the news to him.

He looked even less thrilled.

'I've never had anyone over for dinner in the whole time we've been living here,' I said softly.

'Will you clean your stuff up? And will Eliza go home early so you can get your sleep?'

'Yes, I promise!' I said. I turned to Eliza. 'Do you think it would be OK with your parents?'

'I'm sure it will, but I'll call them just to check,' she said.

I was glad. I felt as if I couldn't present Pegasus to my father and then spend the evening alone with him.

31

'I guess it's all right,' said my father.

I realized that he looked sort of strange, as if he didn't feel well or something. Then I figured out why. There was a letter in his hand – airmail from India. And it was already ripped open.

'Mum wrote us a letter?' I asked him.

'Sort of . . .'

'What did she say?'

'She says,' he said with a deep sigh, 'that she thought she was going to be enlightened by September, but now she thinks it's going to take longer.'

Eliza was staring at him. I'd never told any of my friends that my mother was in India looking for some kind of great wonderful religious something-or-other. She'd been there for a year and a half. She was studying with someone called a lama. I wasn't sure what she'd be like if she was enlightened. Super-mum, maybe.

'Did she say when she was coming home?' I asked, trying to keep the hurt out of my voice.

'Nope.'

'But I'm starting sixth grade in September! And I have the biggest competition of my life coming up! Doesn't she know?'

'I guess she's thinking about other things.'

'Yeah. Great.'

He wasn't finished yet. I could tell there was something else on his mind. 'Speaking of your big competition,' he went on, 'I had a conversation with Rudi today. I called him to see how you

32

were doing, and he told me that he doesn't think you're concentrating enough. Not enough to do as well as you need to in the state competition.'

What! My body hurt all over from concentrating. The only way I could have concentrated enough for Rudi was if I did nothing, day and night, but gymnastics.

I could feel my eyes burning with tears. 'Great,' I said. 'Just great.'

My father tried to soften up a bit. 'I just need you to do a little better,' he said. 'It's so important.'

I didn't answer him.

He reached into the envelope from my mother, which he was still holding. 'Oh, I almost forgot,' he said. 'Your mother sent this for you.'

He handed me a tiny package wrapped in beautiful Indian cotton print fabric. I could still smell my mother's scent on it.

I opened the package. Inside was a small, perfect crystal on a chain.

A tiny piece of paper fluttered to the floor, no more than an inch square. I bent down to retrieve it. A few words were written on it in my mother's neat handwriting: 'May your mind be as clear as this crystal.'

I put the crystal around my neck, thinking that it would be nice if she were there so that I could give her a big hug.

'I'm going to change, and then make us all some dinner,' said my father.

When he'd gone upstairs, I sat back down on the floor with a thump. I was sort of upset.

'Whew,' said Eliza.

'My mum sent me that crystal because she cares about me,' I said.

Eliza just nodded. 'It's OK,' she said finally.

Suddenly, I felt a need to defend my life to her. It's one thing thinking your life is crummy, but it's another thing when somebody else thinks so.

'It's not all that bad, really,' I said. 'My mum is wonderful. You'd really like her. She's funny, and she hugs a lot, and she loves horses, and she sings stupid songs with me. She just needed to go away for a while and . . . find herself. She misses me. She writes me letters from the place she's in. It's sort of a school.'

'Your dad must miss her a lot,' said Eliza.

'It's really hard on my dad,' I went on. 'See, it was nice when my mum was here because she kept him from pushing me too hard. She'd always say, "Give the kid a break, Jeff – she's only a tender young twerp." I mean, I know he loves me, but . . . The thing is, he just cares so much about my winning at gymnastics.'

'Didn't you tell me that your father was a champion gymnast himself, a long time ago?'

'Yeah, he almost made it to the Olympics. But then his father died, and he had to quit and help his mother take care of the other kids.'

'That's so sad.'

'Yeah.' I picked at a long loop on the carpet.

34

'I guess it's sad. But I'm really tired of hearing about it.'

The loop broke.

'Maybe we better not tell your dad about Pegasus tonight,' said Eliza. 'He's not in the greatest mood.'

'I was thinking that, too,' I agreed. 'But I'm afraid my dad might hear him whinnying out there during the night. Then I'd be in *big* trouble.'

'I could sneak him out after supper and take him back to my house,' said Eliza. 'I'm sure it would be all right with my mother, especially if it's just until you can tell your dad.'

There were footsteps on the stairs, and we both jumped to our feet.

My father had changed out of his work clothes and looked as if he was feeling a little better. He still didn't look great, though.

'Well, girls, what'll it be?' he said. 'Chicken Surprise or Liver and Cheese Sauce Surprise?'

'We could cook dinner, Dad,' I offered. 'You should relax. There's a lot of stuff in the refrigerator. I can make mushroom-and-onion omelettes. I'm getting pretty good at that.'

'And I'm great at salads,' said Eliza. 'It's my job at home.'

'Well, I am kind of tired,' said my father. 'You really think you can do this?'

'Absolutely,' I said.

'Great,' he said. 'I'll read the paper. Just holler if you need me.'

Eliza and I went into the kitchen and got busy.

'Where's the cutlery?' Eliza said. 'I'll start setting the table.'

'In that drawer,' I said, pointing. 'Maybe we'll eat in the dining room. It might cheer up my dad.'

Eliza pulled open the drawer and started taking out forks.

'Ow!' She pulled her hand out of the drawer. Her finger was bleeding a little.

'Oh, no, I forgot to warn you about that screw!' I said. 'It sticks out right by the spoons, and it's pointy. Are you OK?'

'I'm fine,' she said, her finger in her mouth.

My father had come running in from the living room when he'd heard Eliza yell. 'I'm sorry, Eliza,' he said. 'I've been meaning to fix that, but Abby and I just kind of got used to it. Let me look at it.'

She showed it to him. It had stopped bleeding.

'I've got to fix that screw right now,' he announced, turning towards the door. 'I'll be right back. I'm going to get my tool kit from the shed.'

Uh-oh

Eliza and I froze. We looked at each other in complete panic. It felt as if the world had stopped turning.

My father was halfway out of the door when we unfroze. We both started jabbering away at the same time.

'Don't get your tool kit!' I blurted.

'I'm fine! You don't need to fix the drawer on account of me!' Eliza stammered.

My father stopped, confused. 'Huh?' he said.

Eliza took control. She just started talking at him, a mile a minute – I'd never seen this side of her before. 'You know, it's the funniest thing,' she said. 'I got a cut exactly like this, last week in my mother's office. Only that cut, um, it wasn't as simple as this cut. See, I was helping my mother give some jabs to a stray dog – my mum's a vet, you know – did you know that? Her name's Victoria Spain, you might have passed her office. And so, anyhow, we were giving these jabs to this dog, and –'

37

While she was talking, she kept glancing over my father's shoulder at me and darting her eyes towards the back garden, as if she were trying to tell me something. Finally, dope that I am, I figured it out. She was telling me to go out the back and get Pegasus out of the shed while she yammered at him.

'Excuse me,' I muttered. 'Gotta go to the bathroom. Be right back.'

I ran to the front door, slipped out as quietly as I could, and sprinted to the shed.

Pegasus was happy to see me. He stamped his feet and shook his mane around. I was pretty happy to see him, too.

'Shh,' I said, stroking him. 'Gotta be really quiet, OK? My life depends on it.'

I pulled the door aside a little so he could come out and slipped the halter over his head.

Now the question was, Where should I put him?

I couldn't put him anywhere outside the house. My father might see him on his way to the toolshed. I had to think very fast, because I didn't know how long Eliza's babbling was going to work.

If I took him into the house and stashed him in a place where my father wouldn't see him, then he could stay there for a little while. Then he could go back to the shed after my father had finished fixing the drawer and put the tools back.

OK. I had a plan. Now all I had to do was make it work.

I led Pegasus quickly around to the front of the house and poked my head in through the front door. Eliza was still talking. Unbelievable.

'– and so, of course, there was no way to know if he had rabies or anything right that second – did you know that there's been an epidemic of rabies around here over the last couple of years? So my mother had to take a blood test –'

The stairs to the second floor were right next to the living room. I figured I'd try to get him up to my room.

No go. He couldn't seem to get the hang of climbing the stairs. And I certainly couldn't carry him by myself! He'd have to stay on the first floor.

Aha! The larder.

The larder was right beside the kitchen, but it had two doors. One went to the kitchen, the other to the dining room.

I opened the door from the dining room and looked around, making sure the door to the kitchen was closed. It was, plus it was a heavy door. It should be pretty soundproof. I led Pegasus into the larder, looped his lead around the hook we hung the apron on, and pushed a large bag of potatoes in front of him. His head stuck out over it. He looked at me questioningly.

'Stay here,' I whispered to him. 'Just for a few minutes. And please, please, *please* be quiet.'

Then I closed the door and ran around to the kitchen.

'Sorry,' I said to them.

'– so, you see, it all ended happily, especially since Mr Grimaldi took the dog. But isn't it funny that now I have a cut on the exact same finger?'

My father was giving her a weak smile. He clearly thought she was the strangest kid he'd ever met. She looked exhausted.

'Oh, you're back,' said my dad. He sounded totally relieved. 'Well, I'll be going out to the tool shed now.' He looked at me strangely, as if to say, 'Who is this weird kid?'

As soon as he was gone, we collapsed against the wall.

'Oh, geez, that was awful!' panted Eliza. 'Where'd you put him?'

'In the larder,' I said, pointing my thumb at the door.

'But that's right here!'

'It's the best I could do on short notice!'

'Well, I guess it's only for a few minutes.'

My father came back with his toolbox.

'Funny smell in the shed,' he said to me. 'I guess some squirrels or something must have got in there.'

He squatted down by the drawer and began rummaging around in his box for the right tools. We stood by, biting our nails in anxiety.

'This shouldn't be any big deal,' he said. 'Just take this baby off, put on a nut and bolt, and –'

There was a small whinny from the larder.

'Did you hear that?' said my father.

40

'Hear what?' I said, trying to keep the horror from my face.

'I didn't hear anything,' said Eliza.

My father had the screw half out.

There was another whinny from the larder, but this time I was ready. I instantly started coughing.

Eliza started coughing, too.

'Are you girls OK?' my father asked.

'Fine,' I hacked. 'Just a tickle in my throat.' We both kept coughing until we couldn't cough anymore.

'Whew,' I said. 'Must have been something in the air.'

My father finished work on the drawer, then closed up his toolbox. 'Good as new,' he said.

He stood up. 'Why don't you let me make dinner?' he said. 'I don't want anybody else getting hurt in here.'

He put the toolbox on the floor by the door and walked over to the sink to wash his hands. I could hear some noise in the larder, but luckily my father was too close to the running water to hear it. I couldn't figure out what the sound was – it almost sounded like paper ripping or something.

'Aren't you going to put your tools away?' I asked my father.

'Nah, they can wait. I'll do it after dinner.'

Eliza and I looked at each other desperately.

'I'll just go get my handy-dandy apron –' my father began, heading towards the larder.

'Oh, no!' yelled Eliza.

'What's wrong?' said my father.

'I don't know – I mean,' she said, looking wildly at me, 'I – I think I have something in my eye. It's really bothering me. Can you look for me?'

'Sure,' he said, throwing me that your-friend-is-strange look again.

As they moved under the light, I scooted back into the dining room and opened the door to the larder. There was Pegasus. His lead had somehow come loose from the hook. He was calmly rooting around in a giant-size box of Cheerios that he had ripped open. He looked up at me, his face covered with stuck-on Cheerios.

'Oh, no, Pegasus!' I hissed at him. 'What did you do? Do you want to get me *killed?*' I frantically started brushing Cheerios back into the box and stuck the box behind the sack of potatoes. Pegasus nuzzled me, as if he knew he was in trouble.

'I guess it's nothing,' I heard Eliza say. 'Thanks for looking. GOSH, I GUESS YOU LIKE WEARING AN APRON, HUH?'

She had to be talking really loud because I was running out of time!

'Yup, I do,' said my dad, opening the door just as I was slipping Pegasus out the other end of the room.

Eek! There was no time to get him out of the house. I had to get him out of sight, fast. Right next to the larder, off the dining room, was the downstairs bathroom. I led him in there, shoved him as gently as possible into the shower cubicle, and closed the frosted glass door on him. 'Just a few minutes,' I whispered to him. 'I promise.'

Then I ran back to the kitchen, where my father was tying the apron around his waist.

'How about if you girls keep working on setting the table,' suggested my father. 'I'll whip up these omelettes.'

As we laid the plates down on the table, we had an almost-silent conversation out of the corners of our mouths. Every time my father glanced over at us, we stopped talking.

'Where is he?' Eliza whispered.

'In the shower cubicle.'

'Oh, no!'

'I can't eat supper with him in there. It'll drive me crazy.'

'He might make a noise.'

'I know.'

'Let's take him back to my house for a day or two.'

'Now?'

'Yes, now. I have a plan.'

'OK.'

Eliza let out a loud and piteous moan. 'Oh, my head,' she wailed.

My father looked over at her, totally startled. 'What?' he asked. 'Your head?'

'Oh, I just got such an awful headache. I get them sometimes. Maybe it was the thing in my eye.'

43

My father looked at her as if she were an alien from outer space.

'Ooooh, it hurts. My head.'

'Stay right there, I'll get you some aspirin,' my father told her. He rushed towards the bathroom.

'No, it's OK!' she yelled. 'Really! I can't take aspirin. It, uh, gives me a stomach ache!'

My father came back into the kitchen and gave me a look that said 'Help!'

'I'm really sorry, but I think I just need to go home and lie down,' said Eliza. 'Sorry to miss dinner.'

'It's OK,' said my dad. 'It's fine, really.'

I thought fast. 'I'll walk Eliza home while you make dinner,' I told him. 'Would that be all right? I just want to make sure she gets home OK.'

'No problem at all,' he said. 'Take your time. Dinner will be ready by the time you get back.'

'Thanks, Dad.' I hugged him.

'Sorry to cause all this trouble,' said Eliza. And I knew she really was.

My father was chopping an onion and crying as we snuck into the bathroom and opened the shower cubicle.

There was Pegasus, his head and neck soaked with water. He had somehow turned the shower on a trickle, and now he was pushing the soap around the floor of the shower stall with his nose.

'Pegasus!' I whispered frantically. 'You're not just going to get me killed, you're going to get us both killed! Or at least put in prison or something!'

Pegasus gave the soap a last push with his nose and sneezed.

'Bless you,' my father called from the kitchen.

Quickly, I dried Pegasus off with the hand towel and pulled him out of the shower cubicle. Then I opened the bathroom door a crack to make sure the coast was clear, and stepped out with him.

Eliza was already waiting outside on the front steps. I led Pegasus through the living room and out.

'Bye, Dad!' I called. 'See you later!'

'Hope you feel better soon, Eliza,' my father called.

'I will,' she said. 'Definitely.'

We closed the door behind us and we were out.

I looked at Eliza in total admiration. 'Wow!' I said. 'I had no idea you could think so fast!'

Eliza shook her head. 'I didn't either,' she said. 'I honestly didn't.'

Stinky and Mike

When we got to Eliza's house, we could hear a ruckus from all the way down the driveway. Little and Archie, the most excitable of Eliza's dogs, were at the window, barking their heads off. Two small and nasty-looking boys were outside the house, looking in through the living-room window. The dogs were going nuts inside as the boys made faces at them through the glass.

'Shoo!' said Eliza. 'Go back to your little cave, or whatever rock you live under.'

The boys turned around to face her. 'We might not feel like it,' said one of them, who had dirty, stringy brown hair and a nose that was pushed up so far that he looked like a pig.

'Yeah, we might not feel like it,' agreed the other one. That one had dirty, stringy blonde hair and glasses. He still had his hands behind him, and was tapping on the window to keep the dogs worked up.

'Get out of here!' yelled Eliza. 'Right now!'

They might have kept arguing, but at that

moment, Eliza's mother came up the path that led from her office at the side of the house. The boys knew the jig was up. They skulked off into the night, giggling to themselves.

'Stinky and Mike,' explained Eliza.

'I thought so,' I said. 'Who else could it be?'

Dr Spain reached us and gave Eliza a hug.

'Hi, Mum,' said Eliza. 'Boy, you're working late.'

'I just had to go over to the office and check on a Doberman with liver problems,' she said. Then she looked down and noticed Pegasus.

'Well, well, what have we here?' she said, bending down to get a good look at him. She had bushy hair and glasses, just like Eliza, and I had never seen her get mad over anything.

'Mum, meet Pegasus,' said Eliza.

'Hi, Pegasus,' said Dr Spain. He pulled his upper lip back at her, and she chuckled as she stood up. 'And hi, Abby.' She knew me well, because she'd had to talk me out of adopting a wild baby raccoon the first time she'd met me.

'Mum,' said Eliza, 'could we keep Pegasus in the back garden for a day or two?'

'Sure. How come?'

Eliza told her mother the story of how I'd found him at Havencrest Stables, and her mother furrowed her brow and clucked. 'I know those people,' she said. 'I've treated their horses once or twice, when they became ill because the Averys didn't take proper care of them. I'm glad you saved little Pegasus here, Abby.'

'Well, here's the thing, Mum,' said Eliza. 'She hasn't quite saved him. Her dad doesn't know about him yet. We have to wait until just the right moment to tell him about it. It's sort of a delicate situation. He wants Abby to do gymnastics all the time and not have any distractions.'

'And Pegasus is sort of a distraction,' I said.

'Hmm, I see,' said Dr Spain. 'Well, I'm happy to let you keep him here. It'll give me a chance to watch him and make sure he's OK. But what if your dad doesn't say yes, Abby?'

'I guess I'll have to come up with a new plan,' I said.

She grinned at me. 'Good idea.'

Dr Spain turned to Eliza and said, 'You'd better put Pegasus into the back garden. Make sure the gate is closed. I guess you'll just have to take responsibility for walking the dogs, instead of letting them out in the garden, until he goes back to Abby's house.'

Eliza kissed her mother on the cheek. 'Thanks, Mum,' she said. 'You're the best.'

Dr Spain went into the house, and we walked Pegasus around to the back.

'Your mother is great,' I said.

'She has her good points. Your mother sounds great, too,' Eliza replied. 'I hope I can get to meet her sometime.'

'Yeah, I hope so, too,' I said.

We put Pegasus into the garden. I could hardly bear to leave him behind. 'Stay here and be good, my little sugar lump,' I said to him. 'Everything's going to be fine, you'll see.' I hugged him and kissed him, and then I went home to have mushroom-and-onion omelettes with my dad.

On Monday I got to the gym early. I was determined to show Rudi that I was concentrating, even though the truth was that it was hard to think about anything but Pegasus. But I really looked good. I put extra energy into the drills, kicking forwards, backwards, and to the side as high and as straight as I possibly could. No slacking off for me. I ran at full steam for 25 minutes. I practised my vaults when everybody else was taking a break. I did extra pull-ups on the bars when everybody else had finished. I was Abby Goodman, Wonder-Gymnast.

My two friends in the class, Andrea and Michele, were amazed and impressed. 'What's got into you today?' Andrea asked me.

'Concentration,' I said through gritted teeth, lifting my legs into a perfect L.

'Not bad,' said Rudi when I was lying collapsed on the floor at the end of the day.

That Rudi. What a fun guy.

I took the bus straight to Eliza's house after practice. I needed to see Pegasus, find out how he was doing, and give him a hug.

Eliza was in the back garden with him, just lying on her stomach and watching him eat grass. She sat up when she saw me.

'I've been hanging around with him all day,' she said. 'I didn't even practise my tuba. Abby, I love him!'

Something about the way she said that made me jealous. After all, *I* was the one who found him. 'Don't love him *too* much,' I said. 'He's mine – all mine.'

'I know, I know,' said Eliza. 'But I do love him. Couldn't he be just a tiny bit mine?'

'Maybe just a tiny bit,' I said. '*Really* tiny.'

Pegasus had trotted over to me and nuzzled his forehead against my front. 'How could they just leave him there to starve?'

Eliza just shook her head.

'People,' I snorted.

I lay down next to her and we both chewed on blades of grass. 'I was thinking,' said Eliza, 'maybe I'll call Lisa and Molly and see if they want to come over. We could have a picnic in the back garden with Pegasus.'

'Yes!' I said. 'That sounds great.'

Eliza got up and went into the house to call Lisa and Molly. I stayed in the garden and watched Pegasus.

In a few minutes, the back door opened from the basement apartment under Dr Spain's office. Out came the hideous Stinky and Mike.

Oh, yuck. They were heading towards me.

'We know something about you,' said Stinky.

'Yeah, we know something about you,' said Mike.

I didn't have a clue how to respond to this.

'My name is Antoine,' said the brown-haired one.

'But they call him Stinky,' said the other one. He snorted with laughter. Stinky elbowed him in the ribs.

'I know, I know,' I said disgustedly.

'And we know something about *you*,' said Stinky.

'*What*?' I finally demanded in exasperation.

'We know you have a secret,' said Mike.

'Yeah, we know you have a secret,' said Stinky.

I was sort of hypnotized by a combination of curiosity and disgust, the way you might be if a big hairy spider was crawling up your arm.

'What do you *think* you know about me?' I said.

Stinky immediately started stroking Mike's head in a particularly nauseating way and crooning to him in a revolting voice: 'Oh, Pegasus, my little sugar lump, you be good or maybe my daddy will find out about you, and we don't want that, do we, my little Peggy-weggy?'

I was so mad I could have easily strangled them both. 'Were you spying on me?' I demanded.

They elbowed each other again. 'We weren't spying,' said Stinky. 'We just happened to be by the window last night when you were talking.'

Yeah, sure. From where their apartment windows were, they would have had to be standing on a chair with their ears pressed to the window to hear us.

'Well, since you happened to be at the window, maybe you heard that I'm going to tell my father about him. I just have to wait till the right time. So you can just butt out.'

'The thing is,' said Stinky, 'the thing is, we were thinking.'

What a shock.

'We were thinking that we might take a walk over to your house right now and have a little talk with your father,' Stinky continued.

'He'd probably be interested to know you have a horse,' Mike added. 'He *needs* to know.'

'No! He has to hear it from me!' I lunged for them, but they leapt clear. They were probably used to getting away from people who wanted to strangle them.

Eliza came out of the house. She gave me a questioning look.

'Wait a second,' I said to Mike, having a sudden thought. A sudden *horrible* thought. 'How do you even know where I live?'

They got identical grins on their faces. They were evil.

'You followed me home, didn't you!'

'It's a free country,' said Stinky. 'We can walk where we want to.'

'Go away,' Eliza said to them.

They kept looking at me. 'So, what'll it be?' said Stinky. 'Should we take a walk right now and see if he's home?'

'No!' I yelled again. That would be a very bad idea, I knew, because he was paying bills today. Bills always put him in a terrible mood.

'We could go see him,' said Mike, 'or –'

'Or what?' I said. Eliza was now watching this scene with her jaw hanging open.

'Or you could give us twenty dollars,' the two of them said as one.

'Get out of here! Right now! I'll have my mother evict you!' Eliza yelled.

'Careful, careful,' said Stinky. 'People always try to evict us, and our mother always sues them.'

They started backing away from us.

'We'll give you a few minutes to think about it,' said Mike. 'You don't have to decide right now. Take half an hour.'

'Yeah, we're not that mean,' said Stinky.

'Scram!' I yelled.

They turned and ran.

'I-yi-yi,' I moaned when they were gone. 'What am I going to do?'

'Maybe we could fry them with a magnifying glass, the way they fry insects,' said Eliza.

'I wish,' I said.

'Molly and Lisa will be here in a minute,' she said. 'Why don't we all talk about it? Maybe we can come up with a plan.'

'OK. 'Cause I sure don't know what to do. I

can't stand the thought of giving them twenty dollars – I don't even *have* twenty dollars to spare, if I'm going to feed Pegasus – but I can't let them go over there and tell my father. He'll be so mad if he thinks I'm keeping a secret from him. He'll just say no, without hearing my side. I have to be the one to tell him, and I have to do it at the right time.'

'The Animal Rescue Squad has twenty dollars.'

'I really don't think blackmail is a very good use of our hard-earned money,' I said.

'Maybe we could lock Stinky and Mike up in a cupboard.'

'They're a couple of moles,' I said. 'They probably thrive in the dark.'

Molly and Lisa came around the back of the house.

'Oh, I'm so glad you're here!' I yelled, running over to meet them. 'We need a meeting. Or something.'

We all sat on the grass and I told them the story of Stinky and Mike, with Eliza adding all the nasty little details I'd forgotten.

'That's revolting,' said Lisa.

'It's probably not even legal,' said Molly. 'I'd like to do some research on this and see if we could have them arrested for blackmail.'

'Great idea,' I said. 'But I don't think there's time right now. I have to figure out how to stop them before they go over and tell my father.'

'We could just give them the stupid twenty

dollars to shut them up,' said Lisa. 'We have it in the treasury. You could think of it as an animal rescue problem.'

'I think maybe if we give them the twenty dollars, it means we're as bad as them. It's almost like we're committing a crime together with them,' I said.

Everybody mulled that one over.

'I guess the question is, is it OK to do bad in order to do good?' mused Eliza. 'We do need to make sure Pegasus gets saved.'

We mulled it over some more.

'What do you think your father would do if you just went home and told him right now?' Molly asked. 'Before Stinky and Disgusting could get there?'

I flinched. 'Wow,' I said. 'Scary.'

'We all could go with you,' said Eliza. 'For support.'

'No, I think that would just make it worse. He'd be mad because he'd feel we were ganging up on him. I think I have to do it alone.'

'You have to tell him sometime,' said Lisa.

'I was waiting for the right time, that's all.'

'There might not be a right time,' said Molly. 'What if he's in a bad mood about this or that for the next two weeks? Are you going to keep sneaking over here and keeping this secret from him? And what if we give Stinky and Mike the twenty dollars, and they decide they want more money tomorrow? Then what?'

I sighed. 'You make much sense, Oh Wise One,' I said. 'I better get this over with.' I stood up.

'But what about our picnic? My grandma packed all this food for us,' said Lisa. She was still holding a brown paper bag full of stuff she'd brought from her house. I could see a banana and two boxes of cookies sticking out of the top.

'Now that I've made the decision, I've got to get this over with,' I said. 'I'm feeling a little sick to my stomach now anyhow. Why don't you guys have a picnic without me? If you have any vegetables in there, especially carrots, give Pegasus some, OK?'

I straightened my shirt. I felt as if I was going off to a war.

'Good luck, Abby,' said Molly.

'How bad could it be?' said Eliza. 'He loves you.'

'It's true,' I said. 'He definitely does love me.' Somehow, this didn't soothe my nerves as much as it might have.

I gave Pegasus a hug and marched out of the yard.

When I was almost at the front of the house, I heard noises behind me. Stinky and Mike raced out of the house into the garden. 'Hey, what about our twenty dollars?' they were yelling.

'Get lost,' said Lisa.

The Deal

I trudged home with heavy feet. I did not want to do what I was about to do. But if I was going to keep Pegasus, I'd have to do it sooner or later. Molly was right.

I could hear papers being shuffled at the dining-room table. 'I'm home, Dad!' I called from the door.

'Good,' he called back. 'I was just starting to worry about you. I wish you'd call me when you're not coming straight home from practice.'

I walked into the dining room.

'Sorry, Dad. I'll try next time.'

He got up from the table and rubbed his eyes. 'Bills are the worst,' he said.

'I know,' I said. 'I'm never going to pay them when I'm a grown-up.'

He laughed. A good sign.

'Want to call out for some Chinese food?' he asked.

'Sure,' I said. 'But order from that place that'll send steamed vegetables and rice, not the one that sends the stuff that drips with grease.'

57

'Definitely,' he replied. 'Careful eating at all times.'

'Yes, Dad,' I said. 'Careful eating at all times' is Rudi's motto. He should have it tattooed onto his forehead. It was drummed into us girls and our parents from Day One. I'm sure he'd like to stand over each one of us and watch every bite we put into our mouths.

'Actually, I'm not really hungry yet,' I told my father.

'That's fine with me. We'll order later.'

'The thing is,' I said, sitting down at the table, 'there's something I need to talk to you about.'

I swallowed, and it felt as if there were a lump of sand in my throat.

He looked worried. 'What's wrong?' It seemed as if he worried a lot more about me since my mother had gone.

'Nothing's wrong,' I said quickly. 'It's just that, um, I have sort of a problem.'

'Something I can help with?'

'Well, yes.'

He sorted through his papers, waiting for me to come to the point.

'Dad, you know I go riding at Havencrest Stables, right?'

'Right.' He looked completely bewildered by this beginning.

I launched right into the story of Pegasus, and how the Averys had left him. I talked about how cute he was, and how little care he needed, and

58

how badly he needed to be saved, and how responsible I was.

'So, what do you say, Dad?' I said, crossing my fingers behind my back.

His mouth was set in a straight line.

'I don't think so,' he said.

'Oh, Dad, *pleeease?* I'll be so good with him, and you'll like him too, and—'

'The answer is no. You've already got too many distractions from your gymnastics. You don't need another one. I put a lot of time and money into your classes. I don't want to see you throw it away – not when we're almost there. Plus which, it will cost too much. I have enough trouble paying the bills as it is. The horse can go to the animal shelter. The subject is closed.' He went back to his papers.

I felt the tears overflow from my eyes and run down my face. Then I stood up without saying anything. The last thing I needed right now was to be near my father. When I got to my room, I slammed the door and threw myself onto the bed, sobbing into my pillow.

How could he be so awful to me? What had I ever done to him? I always did what I was told. I almost never got into trouble, or told lies, or talked back. I tried and tried and tried to please him. And he wasn't even willing to *listen* to what I wanted. Not even to think about it.

My pillow was soaking wet, but I couldn't stop crying. Why wasn't my mother here? Why had she left me all alone with him? He'd been nice when she was here. How could she be so selfish? What kind of mother goes off to the other end of the world to find herself? How could she leave me here to deal with everything on my own?

There was a soft knock at my door.

I didn't answer. I thought if I was really quiet, maybe he'd go away.

'Abby?'

I squeezed my eyes shut.

'Abby, can I come in?'

I sat up on the bed. He wasn't going away, so that meant I had to talk to him.

'OK,' I whispered, hoarse from crying. 'I guess so.'

He opened the door, crossed the room, and sat on the bed beside me. I avoided his eyes. I had to let him into the room, but I didn't have to look at him.

'Abby, I'm sorry,' he began.

'Sure,' I muttered.

'Abby, this isn't easy for me, telling you I'm sorry.'

I looked at him in stony silence. He glanced down at his hands and continued.

'I've been sitting downstairs and thinking,' he went on. 'And here's what I was thinking. You haven't asked me for much in your life. You never wanted lots of clothes or toys. You never had tantrums when you didn't get what you wanted, even when you were a little girl.'

Exactly, I thought to myself.

'And so when you ask me for something, the way you did today, I owe it to you to listen.'

I began brightening up in spite of myself.

'So here's what I think. I think we should try having the horse here—'

I didn't let him finish. 'Really?' I squealed, throwing my arms around his neck. 'Oh, Dad!'

'Just on a trial basis,' he said quickly.

'OK!' I said. 'I know you'll love him and will let him stay forever!'

'Here's my proposal. You keep the horse here in the garden, and you take full responsibility for taking care of him. I'll try to figure out a way to pay for food and vet bills. At the same time, you keep giving gymnastics your full attention. The state competition is next month. I don't have to tell you how important it is to you. If you pick up the points you need, you'll advance to the regionals, and then you can go to the nationals. We'll be on our way.'

'I know, Dad. I'm working hard. Just ask Rudi.'

'That's exactly what I intend to do. You keep working hard on your conditioning and your tricks. I'm going to check in with Rudi every week and see how you're progressing. If you're not, the horse will have to go.'

'OK,' I said soberly.

'But if you keep doing well, you can keep the horse for good. How's that?'

It was a little scary, but it was a lot better than a straight-out 'No.'

He reached out his hand. 'Deal?' he said.

I shook his hand. 'Deal.'

'Now,' he said, 'why don't you go get this Pegasus fellow from Eliza's? I'd like to meet him.'

'Yay!' I said, jumping up. 'You'll love him. You'll see!'

'I'm sure he's very cute. Just don't get too attached to him before the competition is over with.'

'I promise.'

'Now go get him.'

Life with Peggy

So that was the beginning of my new life with Pegasus. I brought him home, not sneaking this time. My father helped me put up a proper door on his stall in the toolshed.

My dad liked him a lot – he even started calling him 'Peggy', which I thought was weird, since he's a boy horse. But I didn't care. I was just glad he was letting me keep him.

I took my father's deal seriously, because I knew he was perfectly serious about it. I went to the gym six days a week and worked my butt off every day.

'You go, girl!' said Andrea, watching me on the bars. She and Michele had been watching me in wonder every day.

'What's got into you?' asked Michele. 'You're burning up the balance beam!'

I explained to them about Pegasus and how I made a deal with my father.

'You have a *horse?*' screamed Andrea.

'Well, he's a little, tiny horse,' I explained.

'Abby,' said Michele firmly, 'we need to go to your house. We need to see him.'

I thought this was a great idea. Since I'd moved here, nobody from gymnastics had come to my house. In my old town, all my friends had been from my gymnastics team. But here, they all lived in different neighbourhoods and went to different schools. It was hard to get together, especially during the school year.

'Come after class today!' I said. 'Pegasus would love to meet you.'

'Will it be OK with your dad?'

'I'll call him,' I said. 'I think it'll be all right with him. As long as he's hearing from Rudi that I'm doing OK in gymnastics.'

When we were done for the day, I called him. He had just got home. I asked him if I could bring home Andrea and Michele. 'As soon as school starts, we're not going to be able to get together,' I said, beginning to make my case.

Amazingly, I didn't even have to use the rest of my arguments. 'You can always bring home your gymnastics friends,' he said.

The way he said it made me think he wasn't nearly as happy for me to bring home my non-gymnastics friends.

'Should I pick you all up?' he offered.

'No thanks, Dad, we'll get home on our own. It'll be fun.'

'OK then, see you soon. I'm making Macaroni and Courgette Surprise for dinner.'

'Dad, I can hardly wait.'

After I'd hung up, I gave Michele and Andrea the good news. We decided we'd all take the bus to my house. 'How will you get home afterwards?' I asked them.

'Why don't we sleep over?' Michele said. 'Then we could all come back here together in the morning.'

'Quick! Call your mum!' Andrea said to her.

As it happened, though, Michele's mother was just walking in to pick her and Andrea up as Michele was dialling her number. We rushed at her, all talking at once.

'Whoa!' she laughed. 'I didn't quite catch that. Can I have an instant replay, in slo-mo this time?'

'*Mum!*' Michele said.

We then backed up and explained a little more slowly what we wanted.

'It's OK with me if it's OK with Abby's father,' she said. 'Have you asked him yet?'

'No, we just thought of it,' I said. 'But he already said it's OK if Michele and Andrea go home with me.'

'Maybe I'd better give him a call,' she said.

I gave her the number and she dialled him. They discussed it for a while. 'I know,' she said to him. 'They tend to stay up giggling and don't get to sleep on time.'

She stood there listening while we all bounced around her. 'Mmm-hmm,' she agreed with him. 'That's for sure. Uh-huh.'

Finally, she got off the phone. 'You can go,' she said.

'Yippee!' we screeched, jumping up and down.

'But—' she said, raising a finger.

'But we have to get to bed and not stay up late,' I said.

'Exactly.'

'And we have to get ourselves ready in the morning.'

'Correct. Clever girl.'

'We will! We will! We will!' we chanted.

'Andrea, you'd better give your mum a call,' said Michele's mother.

'Oops, I forgot,' said Andrea.

In two minutes Andrea's mother had been called, we were packed up, and everything was set.

'Want me to drive you all over there?' asked Michele's mother.

'No thanks,' I said. 'We're going to catch the bus. It'll be fun.'

Michele's mother said goodbye, and we were off. We made so much noise on the bus, I thought the driver was going to throw us off. Luckily, there were only two other people on the bus, and they didn't seem to hate us too much.

We ran the two blocks from the bus stop to my house. Andrea and Michele couldn't wait to see Pegasus.

'Just wait till you see him,' I cackled. 'You won't believe your eyes.'

We ran straight to the back garden and I flung open the door to the tool shed.

There he was, cute as ever. I led him out into the yard.

'Ta–da,' I said. 'Pegasus Goodman.'

They both screamed with happiness and started smothering him with hugs and kisses while I filled his water trough with fresh water.

But suddenly, I noticed that something was wrong. He just wasn't acting right.

I put up my hand to stop them. 'Hold on a second,' I said. 'I have to look at him.'

'Not fair!' said Michele. 'You get to look at him all the time.'

'No, I mean I think there's something wrong with him.'

He was looking unhappy. Every few seconds he'd start biting at his sides, as if something was driving him nuts. What was the matter with him?

'Can we hug him?' asked Andrea.

'I think we'd better be really gentle with him,' I said. 'I don't know what's bothering him.'

'Oh, poor little Pegasus,' cooed Michele, stroking his mane. He nuzzled her front a moment before going back to biting at his flanks.

'Is he sick?' said Andrea.

'I don't know,' I said. 'I hope not. I need to keep an eye on him.'

I knelt down in front of him. 'Hey, cutiepie,' I said softly into his ear. 'You feeling OK?' He just stood there, breathing hard.

My father came into the back garden. 'Hi, girls,' he said.

'Hi, Dad,' I replied. I introduced him to Andrea and Michele. He recognized them from the gym.

'You girls ready for some really great dinner?' he asked. 'My cooking skills are legendary.'

'Sure,' said Andrea, not knowing what was in store for her.

I left Pegasus grazing in the back garden while we went in for dinner. That way I could see him while we ate, because there was a window right next to the kitchen table.

I thought about mentioning my worries to my father, but then I decided not to. I figured he'd just think, 'Oh, great, a sick horse – something else to break Abby's concentration.' He might even make me get rid of Pegasus right away.

I could hardly get down a bite of the Macaroni and Courgette Surprise. This was partly because it was very, very bad – it included tomato sauce, smelly cheese, and possibly peanut butter – and partly because I was worrying about Pegasus. I tried to keep the conversation going with my father and my friends, but my eyes kept wandering to the window.

Michele and Andrea were politely trying to choke some dinner down too, but they were looking out the window with me. Pegasus was still biting at his sides. He looked just miserable.

Finally, it was time to clear the plates.

'Like some dessert?' said my father. 'I could whip

us up something with canned pears and, oh, I don't know, maybe some jam.'

'No thanks,' we all sang at once. 'We're full.'

I was hatching an idea in my head as I loaded the dishwasher. My dad had gone down to the basement to put the big pot away. I turned to Michele and Andrea.

'Hey, you guys,' I said, 'do you want to sleep out in the back garden tonight? We have a tent and some sleeping bags, and—'

'And we could keep an eye on Pegasus,' Michele finished for me.

I could have hugged her for understanding. 'Yeah,' I said. 'I just can't leave him by himself out there all night. Who knows what could happen?'

'Sure,' said Andrea. 'Let's sleep outside. It'll be fun.'

My father came upstairs, and we managed to get his permission. 'But I'm going to be listening out of my window,' he said. 'I don't want to hear you giggling out there at midnight.'

'Who, us?' I said.

'No way!' said Michele.

'Definitely not!' said Andrea.

'OK, OK,' said my father. 'I'll bring the tent up from the basement.'

In half an hour he had helped us get the tent set up, and we had the sleeping bags laid out. We even had a battery-operated lantern for light. My dad went into the house to watch television.

'This is great!' said Michele. 'I've never slept in

a tent before.' We lay there for a few minutes, just listening to the crickets chirp.

Pegasus was just outside the flap, chewing grass. I leaned out the opening.

'C'mon in, Pegasus!' I invited him. I clicked my tongue at him. He looked at me in some surprise. I clicked again, and Andrea and Michele joined in.

'Come on, it's OK,' I coaxed him.

Finally, he stepped delicately over the zipper in the doorway and came in with us.

He stayed in the tent for about half an hour while we hugged him and kissed him, and then it was clear that he needed to leave. For one thing, we didn't want him pooping in there with us. For another, he seemed to want to go outside to eat grass and keep biting his sides.

So we put him back outside and turned the lantern out, and tried hard not to stay up talking for *too* long, until finally Andrea and Michele drifted off to sleep. I couldn't do the same, though. I kept listening to Pegasus outside. I probably slept a little here and there, but I was awake when the sun came up.

9

Pegasus in Peril

Andrea and Michele woke up early, too, so we decided to take the tent down ourselves. What a mess that was! Michele pulled out some important pole or other while I was inside rolling up the sleeping bags, and the whole thing fell down on top of me. By the time we figured out how to work the thing, our stomachs hurt from laughing.

Pegasus didn't seem to be much better, though. I was really starting to worry when it was time to leave. I didn't want Pegasus to be alone all day. But I had to go to gymnastics. There was nothing I could do about it. The three of us shoved down some cereal and my father drove us to the gym.

I tried to clear my mind while I did my exercises, so Rudi wouldn't tell my father I 'wasn't concentrating'. I worked as hard as I could, but I couldn't seem to stop thinking about Pegasus biting himself.

What I was afraid of was colic. I had heard of colic, but I'd never seen it. I knew enough about it to know that it's not like colic in babies. It's serious, and horses can die from it. And I thought I remembered my mother describing a horse she'd had once, a horse that had had colic. She'd said, as I remembered, that it had been biting at its sides and rolling around on the ground a lot.

I spent the afternoon working on a round-off dismount on the balance beam, and I just couldn't get my landing to be solid enough. I was frustrated and dismayed, and Rudi was pushing me hard. I kept thinking about Pegasus. I couldn't wait to get out of there.

The bus home was really slow, and I bounced in my seat all the way to my stop. I needed to be home *now*. I needed to see for myself that Pegasus was all right, that he didn't have colic. I felt all alone and overwhelmed. What if he was really sick? How was I going to take care of an animal all by myself, especially with my father being so mad?

As soon as the bus opened its doors, I jumped down and ran as fast as I could. I didn't stop at the house but ran around to the back to see Pegasus.

He was rolling in the grass.

I ran over to him, and he scrambled to his feet. He rubbed his forehead against me for a moment, and then bit at his side, lay down, and rolled in the grass again.

'Pegasus,' I said softly to him, stroking him to calm him down. 'I'm not going to let you die. Don't you worry. I'm going to take care of you. I swear it.'

I got up and ran into the house. My father

wasn't there. Hauling out the phone book from under the counter, I looked up Eliza's mother's number. I dialled it as fast as I could. My fingers were actually shaking. I don't think I've ever been so upset.

Dr Spain couldn't talk to me, but her assistant said I could bring Pegasus round straight away. I was so relieved – I'd been afraid she might not be able to see me for a couple of days.

Before I left the house, I gave Eliza a call to tell her what was going on. 'I'll meet you there,' she said. 'Five minutes.'

I ran out and put Pegasus's halter on, kissed him on his little face, and we were off.

The walk over to Dr Spain's office seemed to calm him down a bit. He trotted along at my side, and I thought that he was feeling better because of the movement. I didn't stop being scared, though. What if Pegasus really had a bad sickness?

When I got to Dr Spain's office, I found not only Eliza there but Molly and Lisa, too.

'I called the Animal Rescue Squad out for an emergency mission,' said Eliza. 'If you don't need us now, when are you going to?'

I was so happy to see them, I hugged them all at once. Then we sat down in the waiting room and patted Pegasus while a Chihuahua across the room eyed him very, very nervously.

The Chihuahua was only there for some jabs, so we didn't have long to wait. As soon as the little dog was finished, Dr Spain opened the door for us and smiled. 'You might as well all come in,' she said. 'The more the merrier.'

When we got into the examining room, Eliza's mother squatted down beside Pegasus to look at him. We moved as far as we could across the tiny room to get out of her way. 'I'm not going to try putting him on the table,' she said. 'I don't want to get him all scared.'

She gently pulled his upper lip back and looked at his gums. Then she took her thumb and pressed his top gum with it. She watched it carefully. She put her stethoscope on and placed it against his stomach and held up her hand for quiet in the room. She listened hard for a long time, moving the stethoscope around on his belly. At last she stood up. I realized I hadn't taken a breath in about two minutes.

'This little guy has colic,' she said.

I clapped my hand to my mouth. 'I knew it,' I said. 'Is he going to die?'

'Not if I can help it,' she replied, looking grim and determined.

'What do I have to do?' I said.

'You have to say goodbye to him, for now,' she said. 'I'm going to have to keep him here for the night and get some water into his system. His intestines are all blocked up, you see. I'll have to hook him up to some intravenous tubes. I'll probably be able to let you take him home tomorrow, but you'll have to keep walking him a lot and squirting mineral oil into his mouth.'

74

I panicked. 'I have to go to the gym all day,' I said. 'My father will *kill* me if I don't go. How can I take care of Pegasus, too?'

'We'll do it,' Lisa offered. 'We'll walk him back to your house when he's ready and take turns walking him and everything. You don't have to worry about a thing. Right, guys?' she added, turning to Molly and Eliza.

'Definitely,' said Eliza.

'Animal Rescue Squad to the rescue!' said Molly. She saluted me.

'You guys are the best,' I said. 'The very best.'

'Pegasus is the best,' said Molly. 'We're not going to let him down.'

I turned to Dr Spain. 'How did he get this?' I asked her.

'Well, my guess is probably stress,' she answered. 'His life has been pretty stressful lately, hasn't it?'

I thought about everything that had happened to Pegasus in the past week. Suddenly, I felt so bad for him. 'I guess it has been pretty rough,' I said. 'I wanted to make his life perfect, but I guess I couldn't.'

'That's what being a mother is like,' said Dr Spain with a smile.

'He'll get over this, and then everything will be fine,' Eliza said. 'You'll see.'

It was time to go. I hated leaving Pegasus there, but it had to be done. I gave him one last hug, but I could tell he wasn't much interested.

'He'll be lots better tomorrow,' Dr Spain reassured me.

Before we left, I asked her what the charge was going to be. I was braced for a big hit.

'Just think of it as my contribution to the Animal Rescue Squad,' she said.

I couldn't stop thanking her. 'Anytime you need help with cleaning the cages and stuff, just let me know!' I said.

'It's a deal,' she replied.

As the four of us were leaving, we bumped into Stinky and Mike, who were trailing along behind their harrassed-looking mother. We just glared at them. As they went past us, they both stuck out their tongues at the same time.

When I got home, my father was waiting for me. 'Where's Pegasus?' he asked me. 'I went outside to look for you and found you both gone.'

'He's . . . not very well,' I said. 'Eliza's mother is taking care of him.'

'What's the matter with him? Anything serious?' he asked.

'I hope not. It's just' – I took a deep breath – 'a little colic.'

'Oh, great,' he said. 'Oh, brother. Just what we need. A little colic. Crucial competition in two weeks, and the horse has colic. Great.'

'It'll be OK, Dad,' I said. 'The Animal Rescue Squad is going to take care of him while I'm at the gym. I'll keep concentrating. I promise.'

'I hope so,' he said.

I bit my lip.

'Oh, I forgot,' he said. 'This came for you today.' He handed me a thin airmail envelope. I knew just what it was.

'Mum!' I said. I took it from him and ran upstairs to read it in my room.

'I'm starting dinner,' he called up behind me. 'Tuna Surprise.'

'Be down soon,' I promised him.

On my bed, I ripped the letter open slowly, so I wouldn't damage the stamps. I had a whole boxful of pretty stamps from India on my desk. I kept them separate from the letters, which were pressed carefully into a notebook on my bookshelf.

'My darling Abby,' the letter began.

I know you must be disappointed that I'm not going to be there for the beginning of your school year and for your big competition. I want you to know that I'm disappointed, too, and that I'd be there in a second if I felt there was any possible way I could do it. I just can't leave right now, though. It's hard for you to understand, I know, but I'm close, really close, to a whole new way of understanding things, a whole new way of being. And when I get there and I come back to you, I'll be a much, much better mother than I ever was to you before, or I ever could have been if I hadn't gone. If I'd stayed home, I would have been frustrated and empty, and I would have taken it out on you. I couldn't do that.

Maybe you can't understand all this now, but if

you save this letter and read it again when you're older, long after I've come back, I know it will make perfect sense to you. In the meantime, know that I love you. And don't worry about your big competition. I know you're going to do just fine.

Love,
Mum

I smoothed the letter out and put it behind the others in the notebook. It was so hard for me to know how to think about my mother and what she was doing. I felt as if it would be selfish of me to not be happy for her. After all, she had gone to do something that was very important to her. But sometimes I just felt so mad at her anyway. Wasn't it selfish of *her*, to pick up and leave her family just because she wanted to find something or other? And what were we supposed to do while she was gone? What great thing did *we* get to find?

That night, I didn't sleep much again. I kept changing my positions, kicking the sheets into a twisted mess. I was thinking about my mother, and I was worrying about Pegasus. I must have fallen asleep sometime, though, because I had a dream that I had to train Pegasus to do a cartwheel. If he didn't do it just right, he was going to have to go to India. 'But horses can't do cartwheels,' I kept protesting to Rudi.

'He just has to concentrate,' said Rudi.

When my father came to wake me up, I felt awful. My eyes were glued together. My body wouldn't move. My brain wouldn't work.

'Rise and shine!' said my dad cheerfully.

'I'll rise, but I won't shine,' I groaned.

I went through the motions of getting ready for gym, but on the way there in the car I slumped against the door, unable to talk.

'I notice you didn't eat any breakfast. Are you getting sick?' asked my father.

'I don't think so,' I said. *Just worried sick*, I thought.

At the gym, Andrea looked at me funny while we were stretching. 'Do you know you have big circles under your eyes?' she whispered to me.

'I hope my father didn't notice them,' I whispered back.

'How's Pegasus?' Michele whispered.

'He has colic,' I replied. 'He's really ill.'

'Concentration, girls,' said Rudi. We snapped to it.

I stayed tired, and I wasn't doing very well. I saw Rudi frowning in my direction a couple of times. I wondered what he'd tell my father in their next conversation. I'd been working so hard. Was this one day going to blow it for me?

I tried to perk up as the day went on, but I was just too exhausted. I had a couple of nasty slips on the bars because I just couldn't concentrate.

At the close of the session, Rudi gathered us in a circle. 'Now, girls,' he said in his heavy accent, 'leesen to me. School is starting next week, yes?'

We all nodded.

'OK. Because competition is coming, we need extra practice. After school, you come here every day from four to eight. And Saturday all day. OK?'

We were stunned. 'No Wednesdays off, like usual?' asked Andrea.

'Not before competition,' said Rudi firmly.

'But how will we do our homework?' I wondered aloud.

'Homework is not important. Gymnastics is important.'

I thought maybe I'd try telling my teacher that and see what happened. I'd have to stay up late every night studying if I didn't want to flunk out.

At last we were done for the day. My dad had a job in another town that day, so I knew he wouldn't be picking me up. I dragged myself home on the bus, barely able to keep my eyes open.

When I got to my house, I could hear voices from the back – familiar voices. It was the Animal Rescue Squad! I ran to the garden, and there were Eliza, Lisa, and Molly. And Pegasus!

'He's better!' I shrieked. I ran over to hug him. 'When did you bring him over here?'

'My mum let him go at about ten this morning,' said Eliza. 'She said if we kept walking him and squirting mineral oil into his mouth, he should be OK in a couple of days.'

I flopped on the grass in total relief. I realized I was exhausted – probably in worse shape than Pegasus. 'Thank you, Dr Spain!' I yelled to the sky.

'We've been taking turns walking him,' said Molly. 'We walked him around the block a couple of times. The neighbours think he's really cute. Except Mrs Gresham, that is. She yelled at us to keep away from her roses.'

'It figures,' I said.

I crawled over to Pegasus to make a fuss over him, and he nuzzled me.

And that was how we spent the rest of the afternoon – just hanging out with Pegasus in the back garden. My friends showed me how to squirt mineral oil into his mouth with a big syringe, which was like a needle without the needle part. We walked him around the yard until suppertime, when they had to go. Before they left, they promised they'd be back the next day to watch him while I went to gymnastics.

I walked him for another hour after my father and I had supper, and then I left him for the night. He'd be OK until my friends got there in the morning.

I told my father I needed some extra sleep and went to bed early. I snuggled deliciously into my soft pillow, thinking about Pegasus. He was going to be OK. Everything was going to work out fine.

The Crystal Works

Pegasus got completely better, and the days flew past.

School started. Our town was building a new middle school, but it wasn't ready yet. Our class was going to be the last one ever to have sixth grade in the elementary school.

I found that I was in the same class as Molly and Lisa, which was great. But we had Ms Applebaum, which wasn't so great. Ms Applebaum was a tiny little old lady with white hair. Supposedly, she gave the most homework in the school. Anybody who'd been yelled at by her in the hallway (which was everyone) knew she did not fool around.

I was also in the same class with Bobby Delassandro, the cutest boy in the entire world (except, of course, for Brett, who didn't really count). I'd never been in Bobby's class before. He has this soft, curly brown hair and these blue, blue eyes, and I felt as if I was going to faint every time I was within five feet of him. He was sitting three rows away from me. I tried to keep from looking at him every second, but it was hard to stop. One time I snuck a look at him, and he was looking over at me. But then, five minutes later, I snuck another look at him and he was looking at Lisa.

I didn't have that much time to focus on Bobby Delassandro, though, or even on Ms Applebaum's homework. I was too busy worrying about the gymnastics competition. I was getting really nervous about it. I worked and worked and worked, trying to get my routine perfect. There was even more pressure on me than usual to do well. This time, a lot more was riding on it. I knew my father would be watching me very closely.

At last, it was the big weekend. Saturday morning at 5:30, we all piled into a big chartered bus for the two-hour ride to Springfield – girls, parents, Rudi, everyone. We were all totally wired. The night before, I had broken down in complete hysterics over nothing, and now I was just trying to stay calm and not throw up. I was playing with the crystal my mother had sent me. As long as I kept it in my hand, I didn't feel totally out of control.

I was sitting next to Andrea, which helped, because she had a nice serene attitude. 'Hey, it's not life or death,' she said when she saw me clenching my teeth too hard. 'It's only gymnastics.'

My father was sitting in the back with Michele's mother. That was good. I didn't want his nervousness to rub off on me.

We had all woken up when it was pitch-dark

outside. We all had our hair pulled back into tight ponytails, with tons and tons of hair spray to keep every hair in place and out of our faces. We had all applied a little lipstick, cheek colour, and mascara, but not too much.

Every knee on the bus was jiggling up and down.

Finally, we were there. We knew we were going to see a lot of girls we knew, some friends, some not. I knew I'd see friends from my old town, so I was excited.

The team from Pequod was supposed to be really great this year. This was the first time we were going to see them in action. They would be our main competition.

As soon as we were in the changing room, I spotted Jennifer and Jessica from my old gymnastics club. We screamed and hugged each other, jumping up and down, and told each other how much we missed each other.

'Time to get ready, girls,' called Rudi.

We did some stretching, trying to hear the loudspeaker out in the gym. Finally, it was time to go out for the floor exercises. I kept a tight hold of my crystal.

Michele went before me. The beginning of her routine looked really good. But then she did her round-off going into a back hand-spring, something she'd done perfectly a million times before, and she lost her footing and fell when she landed. She kept smiling, picked herself up, and continued her routine. But she was dying inside, and we were dying for her. She'd lose half a point for the fall.

I took off my warmup jacket and got ready to go out there. My dad was behind me, sitting on a bench, and he gave me a thumbs-up just before I went out.

I stood in the corner of the mat, waiting for my music to cue up, bouncing lightly on the balls of my feet. Then I was off.

I did great.

It was one of those times when everything seems to fall into place. The more things went well, the more I knew they'd keep going well. Everything was clean and right. The crowd cheered when I was finished.

The rest of the day went well, but not as perfectly as the floor exercises. I did well on the bars, but had to take an extra step on my landing. That wasn't a big deduction, though. If I kept going this way, I'd get to keep Pegasus.

The team from Pequod really was good. They were going to be hard to beat. Their floor exercises were especially terrific. Their coach looked really mean, though. She yelled at them when they didn't do everything perfectly.

At last it was time for the balance beam, the final event. The balance beam was always the worst part of the whole programme for me. I just couldn't get rid of the last little bit of fear, and fear is a killer on the balance beam.

My mount was a tiny bit off-balance, but I didn't think it would count. I began my routine.

Everything went along pretty smoothly. And then something happened.

I had just gone from a back handspring into a split. I was all the way down in the split, facing the benches, when I caught sight of my father. He was watching me intently, as he always did. It almost looked as if he was *being* me. And suddenly all his words over the years came flooding into my mind: 'It's just that I want so much for you.' 'I just need you to do a little better.' 'We're on our way.' 'We're almost there.'

I stared into the benches. Who was doing this, me or him?

Pssst! Andrea was hissing at me. I snapped out of it.

I finished my routine as if I were in a dream. It was as though I wasn't even there, that I was suspended in that freeze-frame moment during my split for a long, long time. But actually I had only lost a few seconds. My final score on the beam was a 9.6. I knew that would be enough to get me a trophy.

But, strangely enough, I didn't much care. I hardly listened to the announcer as he called the winners up to the stand, starting with eighth place. I was feeling my crystal, thinking that my mother's wish had come true: my mind was finally clear.

'. . . And in fourth place, Abby Goodman,' I heard through my thoughts. I went up to the front to get my trophy. It could have been a fireplace log as far as I was concerned.

'In third place, Jennifer Warren.' That was Jennifer from my old school. I was happy for her as she came up to join me, tears streaming down her face.

Two of the girls from Pequod came in first and second, and Andrea had come in right after me. We all stood there blinking as the flashbulbs went off in our faces.

When the ceremony was over, Rudi gathered us all together and told us what a great job each and every one of us had done, and how proud of us he was. I had picked up more than enough points to move up to the next level and go to the regionals. I should have been ecstatic, but I felt as if I was watching somebody else in a movie. Even the sounds had a strange deadened quality.

I had kept my half of the deal with my father. I'd get to keep Pegasus! But when my father came up to hug me and congratulate me, I could hardly look at him.

I was glad he was sitting with Michele's mother on the way home, because I didn't want to have to talk to him. I didn't even have much to say to Andrea. She could tell I was in a quiet mood, so she didn't pester me.

It was 8:30 PM when we walked in the door, and we were dead tired.

'Should we have a little frozen yoghurt to celebrate?' my dad asked me.

'No,' I said. 'I'm going to bed.' I started up the stairs.

'All right. What's the matter?' he asked me. 'You haven't said three words to me since we left Springfield.'

I stopped on the stairs and shot him a look. 'Nothing,' I said.

'It *should* be nothing. You won a trophy, you can keep your horse, everything's fine. So what's the matter with you?'

'Everything is *not* fine,' I shot back.

'Is it that Mum wasn't there to see you win?'

'No. Well, yes, that's part of it. But mostly it's you. Maybe it's that you *were* there to see me win.'

'What's that supposed to mean?'

'Sometimes I feel like I'm just doing gymnastics to make *you* happy. It's all about *you*, not about me. I can keep my horse, but only if I do well at gymnastics. You're happy now, but that's only because I won a trophy. So what happens when I go on to the nationals? More pressure and more of these stupid deals? Well, I'm not even sure I still want to *do* gymnastics. What do you think of that? What if I just wanted to be a normal kid and have normal friends and do normal stuff? Or what if I liked horses better than working out all the time? Would you still think I was OK then? I don't think so! Because *we* have to do gymnastics!' I started stomping up the rest of the stairs.

'Just a second!' he called after me. 'That isn't

fair! You and I have both put a heck of a lot into your training, and if you quit, you're letting us both down! It's not a decision you can make on your own!'

'Just watch me!' I called back.

I went up to my room and put some underwear, my hairbrush, and a clean shirt into my backpack. I grabbed my toothbrush from the bathroom. Then I came down again.

'I'm going to Eliza's for the night,' I said to my father.

'Does she know you're coming?'

'No. But if I can't stay there, I'll go to Lisa's or Molly's. I don't want to be here tonight.'

'Fine. Go ahead.'

'Fine.' I slammed the front door behind me.

Halfway down the block, I remembered Pegasus. I wanted him with me. I stopped in my tracks and turned around. Going quietly into the back garden, I put his halter on and walked him out to the street. If I was leaving, he was coming with me.

Dad

In five minutes I was standing on Eliza's front porch ringing her bell. Her father answered the door in jogging pants and a T-shirt that had endangered species on it. I didn't know him very well, because he was almost always working at his construction company in town.

'Hi,' I said. 'I'm Abby. Is Eliza home?'

'Sure is,' he said. 'You must be from the Animal Rescue Squad, right?' He looked down at Pegasus and grinned.

'Right,' I said.

He called for Eliza and she came pounding down the stairs. 'What are *you* doing here?' she said. 'I thought you had your big competition today.' She looked down and noticed Pegasus. 'What are *you* doing here?' she asked him.

My chin started to tremble as I told her what had happened. 'Can I stay here tonight?' I asked.

'Sure. Come on in. Oh, maybe we'd better put Pegasus in the back garden first.'

We got him set up in the garden and kissed

him good night, and then we went up to Eliza's room.

'It's after suppertime,' she said to me, 'but we had brownies for dessert. Should we bring some upstairs?'

'No, I can't have —' I started. Then I changed my mind. 'Yeah. I'd love a brownie.'

We brought a plateful up to her room and stayed up until eleven talking. I ate three brownies. I had a stomach ache when I finally went to sleep — but it was worth it.

The next day, we slept late. I was exhausted, not just from staying up late but also from all the gruelling weeks of practice and anxiety. I finally opened my eyes at about noon, and I smelled pancakes cooking downstairs. Eliza had already gone down.

I threw on my clothes and ran down to the kitchen. Eliza and her big brother Pete were cooking breakfast. That is, Eliza was turning over the pancakes and Pete was trying to flip eggshells across the room into the rubbish bin. He was missing most of his shots.

'Hi,' I said, rubbing my eyes.

'Yo,' said Pete, tossing the hair out of his eyes. Pete was kind of cute. Although I preferred Bobby Delassandro, I could see why Lisa had a huge crush on Pete.

'Are your parents home?' I asked.

'No, they both went to visit my great-grandmother

in the nursing home,' said Eliza. 'Pete and I don't have to go because she doesn't recognize us anyway.'

'That's too bad,' I said.

'Yeah, she used to be really nice to us,' said Pete.

'Are you going to go home today, Abby?' asked Eliza. 'If you're staying, you should probably talk to your father.'

'I don't feel like it,' I said. 'I guess I have to go home sooner or later, but I wish I could stay here for a couple of weeks.'

'You know it would be OK with *me*,' said Eliza. 'But I have a feeling it won't work for your dad.'

'You know what I'd like?' I said. 'Maybe Molly and Lisa could come over here this afternoon. We could have a cheer–Abby-up meeting of the Rescue Squad.'

'Great idea,' said Eliza.

After we'd cleaned up from breakfast, we called them. By then it was about two. They both came over about an hour later, after they'd finished their chores at home.

We didn't even try to have a normal meeting. We just lay around Eliza's room, eating grapes and talking. We patted Big, Little, and Archie. Archie kept begging for grapes, but you had to peel them for him or he couldn't eat them.

'The thing is,' said Lisa, talking through a mouthful of at least ten grapes, 'you shouldn't really quit gymnastics all the way just because you're mad at your father. I mean, you really *like* gymnastics, don't you? Wouldn't it be sort of stupid to just totally quit?'

'I don't even know what I like anymore,' I said.

'I think it's the pressure that's bothering you,' said Molly, carefully peeling a grape for Archie. 'Your dad pushes you all the time. Maybe you could still do gymnastics. But you could get him to stop giving you such a hard time about it.'

I thought about it. Lisa was right – I did like doing gymnastics. There would be a great big hole in my life if I didn't do it anymore. But was there anything in between doing it all out and not doing it at all?

I didn't even know if I was ready to give up being a star. But I felt that I was ready to give it a try. There were kids who just did gymnastics for fun – maybe I could be like them. I just needed a break, even if it was only for a while. I was so tired of my father standing behind me every minute and saying 'We're almost there.'

Although I didn't know *exactly* how to solve my problems, by the time I was done hanging around with Eliza, Lisa, and Molly for a couple of hours, everything made a lot more sense. We all had homework to do. Lisa, Molly, and I had four pages of maths homework for Ms Applebaum, and Eliza had to write an essay about current events. So we figured we might as well all work at Eliza's. It was more fun than going home and working separately.

We were all hard at work an hour later when the doorbell rang. Eliza ran downstairs to get it.

A minute later she was back. 'Abby, it's your father,' she said softly.

'Oh, no,' I groaned. 'I don't want to talk to him yet. Can you tell him I'm not here?'

'You know you have to go down,' she said.

'Yeah, I know.'

I put my shoes on and went downstairs. He was on the front porch. Eliza made herself scarce.

'Hi, Dad,' I said without enthusiasm.

'Hi, Abby,' he said.

We were silent.

'Want to come out on the porch swing and talk to me?' he said finally.

I didn't want to talk at all, but I couldn't say no to my dad. We sat down together. But the swing stayed still.

'Did you have a nice night?' he asked me.

'Yes, thank you.'

More silence.

'Have you done some thinking about gymnastics?' he said.

I took a deep breath. 'Yes,' I said.

'Can you tell me what you've been thinking?'

'OK, I will,' I said, ready for a fight. 'I've made a decision.'

'What is it?'

My heart was pounding. 'I've decided that I'm not going to do gymnastics so seriously for a while. I'm not making it to the Olympics anyhow – you and I both know it by now.'

'Well . . .' he began.

'I'm not done yet. The other thing is, just because you were so great at gymnastics doesn't mean I have to be. I need to decide for myself how much I want to do. If I'm going to do it at all, I need to do it for me, not for you.'

I stopped talking. My heart was pounding harder than it ever had before a gymnastics competition. What would he say?

'Are you done?' he asked.

'I'm done.'

'OK,' he said. 'Here's what I need to say to you.'

I braced myself.

'I've been doing a lot of thinking myself,' he said. 'And here's what I've decided. I think you're right. If I keep pushing you about your gymnastics, you might quit – just walk away and never come back. I've seen it happen. And I don't want you to do that. You're too good, and you have too much fun doing it. It's hard for me to back off, but I'm going to try.'

'Really?' I said, unable to believe what I'd just heard.

'Really,' he said. 'If you just want to go one or two days a week, that's OK with me. Whatever you want.'

I broke into an ear-to-ear grin. Then it immediately disappeared. 'What will Rudi say?' I fretted.

'I'll deal with Rudi.'

I put my head on my father's shoulder and started the swing going. 'I really wanted to stay mad at you.'

'I know,' he said.

We swung for a few minutes.

'Want to come home?' he asked.

'I think so.'

'Why don't you go and get your stuff?' he said.

He waited on the swing while I went upstairs and gathered my things. I thanked Eliza for letting me stay over at her house.

'Anytime,' she said.

I said goodbye to everyone and ran out the back to collect Pegasus. As always, he was glad to see me.

My father and I walked home slowly, with Pegasus clopping along beside me. We talked about gymnastics, and school, and horses, and my mother.

'Are you mad at her?' I asked him. 'Because I am. I try not to be, but I am.'

'I try not to be, too,' he said. 'But deep down, I suppose I am. But we wouldn't be mad at her for leaving if we didn't both love her.'

'I guess that's true,' I said.

When we got to our house, I headed towards the back garden to put Pegasus away. 'Hold on a second,' said my father. 'I just have to check something out back.' He went on ahead of me.

'OK,' he called from the back garden. 'Come on back now.'

Confused, I walked Pegasus around the house to the garden. And when I got there, I was even more confused. There was my father standing beside Brett, the handyman from Havencrest Stables.

'Hiya,' said Brett.

'Brett!' I exclaimed. 'How are you – I mean, what are you . . .'

'Your father called me up, so I came over,' he explained with that crooked little smile of his.

'Oh,' I said, still not understanding what he was doing there.

'Take a look at the shed,' said my father.

I looked across the garden to the shed. I couldn't believe I hadn't noticed it before. It was totally transformed.

First of all, it was a different colour. It had been painted a dark green, with white trim. All the broken bits had been fixed, and it looked like a cute little house. There was even a new window.

I stepped inside the shed. It was a lot lighter now because of the new window. I could see that the inside had been fixed up, too. There was a little stall for Pegasus, made of sturdy wood, and a whole set of grooming tools hanging on the wall.

I raced out of the shed. 'Holy cow!' I shouted. 'It's gorgeous!'

'Take a look over the door,' suggested my father.

I looked. There, above the door, was a sign, painted in fancy lettering, that said PEGASUS.

I ran across the garden and leapt into my father's arms. 'Oh, Daddy, this is exactly what I wanted. I'll never ask for anything else – ever again!'

'Of course you will,' he said with a grin. 'Now, shall we have a little dinner? Brett has to leave soon, so we need to get moving. I made Eggplant Surprise.'

I gulped. 'Cool!' I said, trying to sound enthusiastic.

We sat down to eat. The Eggplant Surprise wasn't too terrible, if you didn't mind the taste of charcoal.

'So, where are you working now?' I asked Brett as I pushed my dinner around my plate.

'Actually, I've decided to go back to college. I'm going to be a vet. I'm working part-time at a feed store to help pay for college. And to save up for my wedding.'

'Your wedding?' I felt myself go red. I hate it when that happens.

'Yup.' Luckily, he didn't seem to notice. 'I'm marrying my girlfriend from high school. She's going to be a vet, too. We might work together one day.'

'That's terrific,' said my father. 'I wish you the best of luck. It has to be better than working for the Averys.'

'You can say that again,' Brett agreed.

'I wonder where they are, those creeps,' I said.

Brett pulled a newspaper clipping out of his shirt pocket. 'My cousin in Albany sent me this,' he said, unfolding it and handing it to me.

COUPLE ARRESTED FOR BAD CHEQUES, it read. It said that the Averys had been put in jail for writing thousands of dollars of phony cheques. They had a barnful of starving horses that had been adopted by several local horse farms.

'Whew,' I said. 'I hope they never own horses again in their lives.'

'Me, too,' said Brett. 'I'll be on the look-out for them, you can be sure of that.'

There was a banging at the kitchen door beside us, and there was Pegasus, pushing at the screen door with his hoof.

I laughed. 'You can't come in, silly,' I told him.

My dad laughed, too, especially when Pegasus banged on the door again. Finally, my father got up and opened the screen door for him.

'OK,' he said, laughing, 'but just this once. Got that?'

Pegasus clip-clopped into the kitchen, took a look around, and headed for the larder.

My father chuckled again. 'He's sure figured out where the food is,' he said.

If he only knew, I said to myself. I ran to fetch Pegasus, and before I brought him back I whispered into his ear: 'Don't you ever tell him you were in here before, OK?'

My dad gave Pegasus a sugar lump from the bowl on the table. 'All right, little guy,' he said, scratching him behind the ears. 'Time for you to go outside now.'

The three of us went outside with Pegasus. The sun was starting to go down. We stood for a little while under a tree in the back garden, watching Pegasus run and play until it got dark.

The Best Letter of All

September 24

My darling Abby,

Well, I think I've finally learned what I came here to learn. I finally understand what I need to do.

What I've learned is that I'm supposed to be at home with my family. I came here to find myself, but I was really running away. I've realized that enlightenment for me isn't about sitting around on a mountaintop waiting to 'get it'. It's about living every day with the family that I love, trying to be helpful, and trying to be a good person to the people I love — you and your dad.

So what this means, my honey-bunch, is that I'm coming home to you. I'm packing up all my stuff tonight, and I should probably be home a day or two after you get this letter. I can't wait to see you.

Love and kisses,
Mum

About the Authors

ELLEN WEISS and MEL FRIEDMAN are a husband-and-wife team who have written many popular books for young readers, including *The Curse of the Calico Cat, The Adventures of Ratman, The Tiny Parents*, and *The Poof Point*.

They live in New York with their daughter, Nora, and their boxer, Gracie. Over the years they have taken in many stray animals, among them dogs named Big, Little, and Archie.

Don't miss the other exciting books in
The Animal Rescue Squad series starting with:

THE ANIMAL RESCUE SQUAD
Kitten Alert!

By the time we'd made it all the way to the bottom
of the cliff, the rain and wind were so strong that it
looked as if the air was full of blowing smoke. How
would we ever find a kitten in this?

'Listen!' said Lisa.

There was a tiny, tiny mewing. You could just hear
it on the wind.

'Where's it coming from?' Abby asked.

'There,' said Lisa, pointing. We ran down the beach
and stood below a little chink in the rocks – not
even a cave, really – that was about eight feet above
our heads.

'Sebastian!' yelled Molly.

'Mew!' We could just see his little face, peeking out
over the edge above us.

£3.50

ISBN 0 09 971891 X

Colin Dann
THE
CITY CATS
SERIES

By the author of the award-winning
THE ANIMALS OF FARTHING WOOD

King of the Vagabonds
Sammy's survival instincts are put to the ultimate
test when he strays into the dangerous wilds of
Quartermile Field - where he is to be crowned...
King of the Vagabonds.
ISBN 0 09 921192 0   £3.50

The City Cats
Sammy and Pinkie are enjoying their new life in the
big city. Pinkie's expecting kittens and proud Sammy
is top cat of the neighbourhood - but how long will
their good life last?
ISBN 0 09 921202 1   £3.50

And coming soon!

Copycat
When there's a purge on the stray cats and dogs in
the city of London, Sammy and Pinkie find
themselves in the middle of a life or death situation...
ISBN 0 09 21212 9

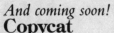

Bumwigs and Earbeetles
and other Unspeakable Delights

Poems by ANN ZIETY
Illustrated by LESLEY BISSEKER

Think ghastly! Think grisly! Think grim! BUMWIGS AND EARBEETLES is all those things... and worse!!!

Smelly socks, crumbly compost heaps and mangy moggies are among the unthinkable, unspeakable delights in this collection.

Catch a whiff of this...

MY DOG NEVER HAD FLEAS

he had bumwigs and earbeetles
and sinus larvae
and one or two exaggerated boils
and bits of ticks that stuck to his ears
and sticky mites
and bites from fights
and stashes and stashes of nasty rashes
but he never had fleas
not one

Coming soon!
RED FOX paperback, £3.50 ISBN 0 09 953961 6
Out now!
BODLEY HEAD hardback, £8.99 ISBN 0 370 31975 3